Praise for Samar Yazbek

"One of Syria's most gifted novelists."
CNN

"Yazbek's is the urgent task of showing the world what is happening. Thanks to her, we can read about the appalling things that go on in secret, underground places."
The Guardian

•

Praise for Planet of Clay

"The Syrian writer Samar Yazbek evokes the horror of civil war with gripping lucidity in her novel *Planet of Clay*."
Le Monde

"With the brazenness typical of her recent work, Samar Yazbek immerses us in the horror of the Syrian conflict, and the way it resonates in the flesh and minds of those who are living it. It is through the women the author has met on the ground throughout this war that she describes the capacity for resistance in the face of atrocity."
Libération

"An ingenious character and a literary approach on the verge of the unimaginable. Samar Yazbek's novel is brave on many levels."
Göteborgs-Posten

"*Planet of Clay* is a deeply original, almost surreal fantasia, written in a simple, clear style. But the evil and the suffering surrounding Rima are so very real. A novel like *Planet of Clay* filters through all our conscious and unconscious blinkers."
Arbetarbladet

"We others can only read—and cry."
Kristeligt Dagblad

"The book left this reader very touched, beyond the cruel reality it describes, thanks to Yazbek's sense for detail."
Weekendavisen

"An invaluable voice from Syria."
Dagens Nyheter

"The text is true—literally true, that is. How can you truly describe rational chemical warfare? By

letting the process supporting the meaning of the text break down. A radical and visionary move made by Samar Yazbek."
Sveriges Radio

•

Praise for A Woman in the Crossfire: Diaries of the Syrian Revolution

"Amid the horrific news about Syrian dissidents, mass killings, and government claims of terrorists, this unique document, written in the first months of the uprising, is a chronicle both of objective events and the visceral and psychic responses of an impassioned activist and artist. The book weaves journalistic reporting into intimate, poetic musings on an appalling reality."
Publishers Weekly

"An essential eyewitness account, and with luck an inaugural document in a Syrian literature that is uncensored and unchained."
Kirkus Reviews

"A feverish, nightmarish, immediate account."
The Guardian

"An impassioned and harrowing memoir of the early revolt."
New York Review of Books

"In her book, *Woman in the Crossfire: Diaries of the Syrian Revolution*, Yazbek shows the reality of what's happening there and brings us stories of many people who risk their lives in the struggle for freedom. The insight that she offers into the complex and bloody conflict is both incredibly valuable and inspiring."
PEN Transmissions

"The best account of the revolution's early months."
The National

"Arresting, novelistic prose. Uncompromising reportage from a doomed capital."
The Spectator

"The heartbreaking diary of a woman who risked her life to document the regime's brutal attacks on peaceful demonstrators."
The Inquirer

plex web of constellations built on discretion, racial hierarchies, financial interests, and abuse."
Asymptote Journal

"This is a book that is deserving of careful attention, by an author who bears following."
Critics At Large

•

Praise for The Crossing: My Journey to the Shattered Heart of Syria

"A powerful and moving account of her devastated homeland. It bears comparison with George Orwell's *Homage to Catalonia* as a work of literature. Yazbek is a superb narrator. One of the first political classics of the twenty-first century."
The Guardian

"Extraordinarily powerful, poignant and affecting. I was greatly moved."
MICHAEL PALIN

"Brave, rebellious and passionate. Yazbek is no ordinary Syrian dissident."
Financial Times

"An eloquent, gripping and harrowing account of the country's decline into barbarism by an incredibly brave Syrian."
Irish Times

"Gripping. Does the important job of putting faces to the numbing numbers of Syria's crisis."
The Economist

"Samar Yazbek's searing new book about her Syrian homeland is a testament to the indomitable spirit of her countrymen in their struggle against the Assad regime. Shocking, searing, and beautiful."
Daily Beast

"Gripping."
Washington Post

Planet of Clay

Samar Yazbek
Planet of Clay

Translated from the Arabic
by Leri Price

WORLD EDITIONS
New York, London, Amsterdam

Published in the USA in 2021 by World Editions LLC, New York
Published in the UK in 2021 by World Editions Ltd., London

World Editions
New York / London / Amsterdam

Printed by Lake Book, USA

This book has been selected to receive financial assistance from English PEN's
PEN Translates programme, supported by Arts Council England. English PEN
exists to promote literature and our understanding of it, to uphold writers'
freedoms around the world, to campaign against the persecution and imprison-
ment of writers for stating their views, and to promote the friendly cooperation
of writers and the free exchange of ideas. www.englishpen.org

The two Qur'an verses on page 140 are Surah Yusuf 11–12, translated into English
by Muhammad Asad, first published in 1980 by Dar Al-Andalus.

Library of Congress Cataloging in Publication Data is available

ISBN 978-1-64286-101-3

First published as *Al Macha'a* in 2017 by Dar al-Adab in Lebanon.

Twitter: @WorldEdBooks
Facebook: @WorldEditionsInternationalPublishing
Instagram: @WorldEdBooks
YouTube: World Editions
www.worldeditions.org

Book Club Discussion Guides are available on our website.

I DON'T KNOW if you care how the paper feels, or whether you are like me and run your fingers over its surface, and it is no use adding anything else about my fingers and how I trace them over the lines my hands have written.

I am thinking something now, and it is that if every sheet of paper piled up in these cardboard boxes were laid out flat, they could make a paper aeroplane the size of the plane circling over my head. But don't think that my worries might mean much to anyone but me. Everything I'm writing you could vanish, and it will be a strange fluke if you have the chance to read it, like the fluke that made me so different from other people.

I was born, and I can't stop walking. I stand up and I set off and I keep walking and walking. I see the road, and it has no end. My feet take over and I walk—I just follow them. I don't understand why it happened, and I'm not expecting you to understand either. This enchantment of mine doesn't care what people might understand.

If you want a good way to get rid of the aeroplane's roar, you can try this. Take a blank piece of paper—do it gently, don't let the pile collapse, take it out like it's an artery. Then put it on a hard surface. Personally, I turn over the coffee tray and make it into a desk, then I pick up the blue pen which I found among the stacks of paper, and I begin. You must not set off before the sound has started. Don't stop unless you are faint from exhaustion, but it must be exhaustion and not fear. If all this isn't done properly, I mean using the blue pen to play with words on a blank page, then my instructions will fail, the blank page won't like you, and the roar of the aeroplanes won't disappear.

Don't think I'm afraid. I don't know who you are, or even whether anyone will read these words. Maybe all this doesn't mean much to you right now, because you don't know me yet. Please don't get annoyed at all my digressions, I didn't study in school like most children do, but I read every book that came my way, even if I learned it by heart without understanding it. There were many books I didn't understand, and Sitt Souad used to burst out laughing when she saw me opening the huge leather-bound books and squeezing my way into them, especially the books on art history.

I think I am one of the many mistakes I've seen God overlook from time to time, or perhaps there is some cruel wisdom of His behind it. I've already mentioned it, but maybe I should remind you, my brain is in my feet and there isn't a thing I can do about this curse. When I was younger, I used to have a dream that they would let me walk and walk until I passed out. I just wanted to try it, so I would know where my feet would lead me.

My mother told me that they discovered it early on. I'd hardly stood upright before I rushed forward. It's so strange! But you have to believe me. They thought I had some sort of mental problem, but the doctors confirmed that my brain was fine. My mother refused to put me in a mental hospital. Everyone called it the hospital for crazies. They were afraid of me but I didn't care, I hated dealing with the outside world, and I found no use in moving the heavy muscle inside my mouth called a tongue.

I knew that I couldn't stop walking, but I'm not sure when it was that I realised. I don't remember when I first recognised colours either, or the moment when I found out I had a nose, or two lips *like a pistachio nut*, my mother used to say. I'm also not sure when I was first tied. Whenever we went out, my mother would place my right hand into hers and tie the two hands together with a rough cord or a rope. But when she was working, she would tie me in a different way. She would cry while she did this. But she never stopped doing it, until the day she disappeared. I will tell you how she used to tie me.

I can remember the moment they found out that my head is in my feet. At the time I was four years old and I used to go with my mother to the school where she worked. I would be tied in the cleaners' room. My mother was responsible for cleaning the toilets and the classrooms and she prepared coffee and tea for the staffroom and the headmistress's office. The school was in the middle of Damascus. We needed to take two buses to reach it from our house, which was at the end of Jaramana Camp in southern Damascus. I am happy for you if you haven't heard of it.

The day she realised I couldn't stop walking, my mother had locked the cupboard drawers in the cleaners' room, untied the cord, and reached out to tie my hand to her wrist, when she gasped and turned away as if she had forgotten something. Adjusting her head covering, she disappeared outside. She was only gone for a few moments, but in that time my feet began to walk forward quickly. What was it I did outside the iron school gate? I don't know, but my mother had hardly unfastened the rope when I felt wings sprouting between my toes, and I turned towards the street. In a few minutes I was part of another world. I wasn't tempted to cry, I followed my feet very happily. You have to understand that I was walking on the road and the pavement in a straight line, and I didn't take any notice of my surroundings until a group of people formed a circle around me, and took hold of me. My legs didn't stop moving, and I didn't scream. They asked me my name and what my family was called, and at that moment I lost the power to speak—or so I believed, because I couldn't remember my voice, and I couldn't remember anything except how to chant, to recite the Qur'an using *tartil*. I was looking at their mouths circling me, like little holes in a wall. I couldn't tell how much time passed before I suddenly found my mother standing there, wailing and crying, and she lifted me up into her arms. I was so skinny that the people thought I was hardly three years old. She hugged me and rushed me away. She never spoke about what had happened or tried to persuade me to speak, but after that we spent four years going from doctor to doctor as she tried to understand my condition. Since then, I lost my voice altogether and I only hear it when I am reciting the Qur'an. And that is another story I will tell you.

Don't think that what you are reading is a novel. What I'm writing is the truth, and I am doing it to try and understand what happened.

Our life went back to normal, and I kept going out attached to my mother, but after that day when she realised I couldn't stop walking, I began to spend time in the room of the lady who looked after the school library while my mother was working. Everyone loved my mother and they all wanted to help her. She had a kind of humble fragility about her, and a silence too. She was beautiful, but a delicate moustache sprouted over her lip. My mother was shy and barely spoke. She walked with her head bowed, so that I saw a hump grow at the top of her back and get bigger as the years passed. My mother was calm and kind to the point that it made you angry, and I would try to annoy her on purpose so she would shout and I would see her eyes flashing and gleaming. I failed, most of the time. Imagine having a daughter like me—you would probably lose your mind! My mother never told me where my father disappeared to. She suddenly said one day that he had gone abroad, and then she never mentioned him again. This was the same year she discovered that I couldn't stop walking and wouldn't talk.

My life changed in the school library, from that year until I became good at writing my letters. I stayed in that room for years and I never stopped walking, I would go round and round under the eyes of the librarian, Sitt Souad. She cared more about me than any other person in my life. Sitt Souad is another story I will tell you. There are many stories you will hear, if I live. The important thing now is that I tell you how my mother disappeared.

When I got older and my monthly cycles started, my mother decided I should stay at home to protect my honour. I put a covering on my head, a colourful hijab. I would fix it in the shape of a rose, which made me laugh and feel happy. My mother began to tie me to the bed in our room with a long rope when she went to work. The summer months we spent together.

My brother was two years older than me and studying at the university; my mother and I didn't see much of him. Our house was made up of a single room, and there was a kitchen and toilet inside. We used to wash ourselves in the kitchen. My mother moved as if she was being watched all the time, I was born with legs that led me forward and I lost my voice, and my brother was constantly angry, though recently he had seemed even more irritable than usual. On the television, we would hear them talking about gangs who went about robbing and murdering people. My brother would say *Liars*, and my mother would shout at him to be quiet.

That day, when my mother disappeared, I didn't know what was going on. Life seemed to be snapping at our heels. I had started to hear planes roaring overhead, our neighbours were disappearing, and men in normal clothes and military uniforms would burst into people's houses. This was called a *security patrol*. I saw all this but I didn't understand.

My bed was beautiful, and I slept in it with my mother. As long as I could remember, I had lived in a corner of it. In the chest underneath, I hid books from the library and the large Qur'an with gold printing which I had learned by heart. This was everyday life. The rope my mother used to tie me with was long enough for me to move around the whole room. I could reach the window and lean my head out however I liked. When my mother and brother left the house, they would lock the door. I hated the spongy cushions and the mat and I would always sit on my bed. It was my whole world, and I cleaned it several times a day. I washed its sheets by hand. On top of it were two large cushions, along with a smaller triangle-shaped cushion that slept in my lap. It was green with red flowers embroidered on it, and at night I would arrange it under my feet, which, if you remember, had their own mind that was a mystery to me.

The bed wasn't copper. It was made of wood, and it was huge and strong. I used to jump up in the air and throw myself on top of it. Between the mattress and the wooden trunk below, I would hide my pages, and my coloured bags, and my favourite pictures, which my mother refused to put on the wall. My own special box sat in the space between the bed and the corner of the wall, and inside it I kept presents from Sitt Souad, like books and pens and colours. I will tell you about this box later, and also about the books and the pens and the cloth flowers. I didn't use the iron cupboard that my mother used. I put my clothes in a wooden trunk next to the bed on the side facing the wall. I didn't own many clothes, actually—I had a lot of colourful pyjamas. My mother would buy them from Souk Al-Haramiya, a cheap market for second-hand clothes. I would sleep in them for a few weeks, and then turn them into rags to clean our house. My mother usually bought shabby pyjamas, but it wasn't important because I always loved how colourful they were.

The day she disappeared, my mother and I were on a small white bus, and we had stopped at one of the checkpoints. As usual, a thick, short rope, no more than a few feet, was tied between my right hand and my mother's left hand. I was sitting by the window of the bus, and everything around me seemed strange. It had been over a year since I had last left the alley where I was born. I was supremely happy because we were visiting Sitt Souad—she had asked me to come with my mother. Those visits were the most important things that happened to me, especially the journey there.

You can imagine the strange smells which came from the bus. There were body smells, and the summer was hot, and when we opened the windows a warm breeze blew over us. I found myself looking ahead when the bus stopped for the second time. My mother said it was a large checkpoint. Two passengers got off the bus—one of them said it was quicker to walk these days. There were three more checkpoints ahead of us and we had to cross them all to reach the centre of Damascus, where Sitt Souad lived. Her house was close to Al-Najma Square, not far from the school. I had never seen checkpoints before the protests started. I didn't really take much notice of them and I wasn't curious to know more about them even though they were people's main activity. The checkpoints were different from one place to the next. It cheered me up a bit that more people were starting to use bicycles. There used to be a bike that my brother used when he was working as a waiter in Bab Tuma, and I would take a lot of care over cleaning it and making it beautiful, tying coloured ribbons around the wheel. Then I outlined a little picture and put it on the side of the handlebars. The picture was the size of my hand and I drew five feet on it, and three ropes in different colours, and a blue hand. I glued it around

the edge of the wheel to protect my brother
—he didn't really care, but he didn't complain.

So, I was by the window. We are going back
to the checkpoint story.

Through the window I was watching people
ride bicycles, and I envied them. I was thinking that if only I was allowed to ride one, it
would be all I could ever wish for—passing
the checkpoint was much easier for the
cyclists as they didn't have to stop in the
long queue of cars—when we heard a scream.
The checkpoint was directly in front of us.
No doubt you know what a checkpoint is and
there is no need for me to explain it to you,
although the relationship between a word
and its meaning occupies me a lot. Around
the checkpoint I could see a group of men, all
different ages, some of them wearing military uniform and others in normal clothes.
My mother said that the men in normal
clothes were from the National Defence
Army. These groups had been set up recently
to watch people and ensure their safety. That

is what they said on the television. My brother said they were a bunch of mercenaries, and my mother shouted at him to shut up. She shut the windows, grabbed him by the hand and went into the kitchen, which is a way of saying they went through the curtain that divided the room into two parts. One of my favourite games used to be testing kitchen knives by making square holes in this curtain. It was made of a rough material, with plastic on one side and fabric printed with coloured squares on the other. I would use the knife to cut out the red squares so I could collect them. This made my mother so furious that eventually she hid all three of our knives. She never discovered where the squares were, and neither did my brother until one day he ran his hand over his bike, which was covered with coloured squares, and he looked at me and winked. The next day he brought me sheets of red stickers and a small pair of scissors. So, I was looking at the two of them through the holes I had made while they were muttering behind the curtain. I knew they were fighting. My mother was trembling and holding my brother's wrist and staring at him, and her eyes were red from crying. I became distracted by the moving points of light, the results of my square holes, which wavered on the opposite wall like a flock of birds. When I drew back from the curtain, my brother was slipping away silently and his eyes looked odd, like they belonged to a wax doll. Now, we were in front of one of the checkpoints which caused those fights between my mother and my brother. It seemed that this checkpoint belonged to the *Mukhabarat* and the National Defence Army. What did all these names (which were constantly repeated in front of me) mean? I didn't understand, but they all carried weapons.

My mother hung on to me, the men didn't leave their seats, the driver turned off the engine. No one could move. There was a line of cars behind us, and more buses and cars in front of us. The street was crammed with cars and buses and trucks. A long, endless line. A river of cars. Despite the noise, I could hear a sound from the front of the bus where the driver was sitting: *tick tack tick tack*. It came from the steering wheel, which was covered with blue beads, and with every movement and *tick tack* the pendant dangling from the wheel would swing, and at the end of the pendant hung a glass ball with silver stars twinkling inside. I was watching the ball, and my mother had put her arms around me. We heard the scream but didn't understand what was happening. Whatever it was, it was not likely to affect my mood—I was going to see Sitt Souad, and I was watching silver stars float inside the ball hanging from the steering wheel. But the screaming got louder. A woman appeared, howling and tearing at her hair. Facing her were two men wearing military uniforms, and two others in normal clothes carrying huge guns. I didn't know what kind they were but they were deep grey this time, not dark green or black. The woman was kneeling at the feet of two of the men and screaming, and the other two were removing the cotton jacket of a young man nearby and covering his face with it. His body was showing, all the way down to his stomach. One of them hit him with the rifle butt, and do you know what? It was the first time I had seen something like that, and I didn't look away, and neither did my mother. We were staring, and so was everyone else. We watched in silence as the skinny young man who had fallen to the ground turned into a ball under the feet of the two men. He was shouting loudly. The woman had fainted and fallen down and we saw a group of women come near and speak to the men, and they stopped hitting the young man and instead they picked him up and dragged him, and one of them shouted *You son of a bitch!* The young man's head was dangling. His eyes were open and glassy, he didn't answer or react at all. His face was right in front of us now and I could see him through the glass as he started to cry, before the two other men came and picked the rest of him up. The four men carried him by four corners, by hands and feet, and opened the boot of the car. They threw him inside and he let out a high-pitched scream, then they closed the boot and we heard a strange noise. I didn't know what it was, but a huge-bodied man wearing normal clothes was staring at his identity card and shouting, before he got into the car where they had put the young man and they all drove off.

An hour later, it was our turn at the checkpoint. The inspection was necessary. We almost held our breaths, we had been so silent after the car left. I was moving my head quickly from side to side, and my mother hugged me and whispered *Don't be afraid*. I wasn't afraid, I was just trying to memorise the pictures. When the head of a military man popped into the bus, I stopped moving and looked at him. I smiled at him. He smiled at me. I began to bob my head towards him, and he shouted. I stopped moving, and my mother told him I was mad.

He asked for our identity cards and scrutinised everyone's name. He was very grumpy when he examined ours.

I wanted to jump out of the window but I stuck out my tongue instead, seeing as they believed I was mad anyway and it was a good opportunity to do it. My mother put her hand over my mouth and I screamed. The man glared at me for a while. The man standing by his side asked him to leave us be. This second man was nice; he was a soldier too and he carried a huge rifle, the biggest I had seen in my life. The barrel was pointed towards us and I was afraid. The man let us pass.

It took another hour to arrive at the second checkpoint, and it dragged. My mother irritated me when she pulled me roughly towards her. I didn't move. She was trying to hide me in her chest. Cars surrounded us on all sides and the bus moved slowly. I was almost suffocating. I was thin but my chest was large, and I didn't understand why this weight made me feel I couldn't breathe; I felt like strings of water were pouring over my stomach. I was suffocating in the head covering I had fastened with two red pins, and my jeans, and the shirt which reached my knees; the rope tying me to my mother was scratching and burning me. My mother had tied it very tight before we left the house and even though it was made of fabric, it made my skin sweaty and itchy. I wanted to scream, but I couldn't. I wanted to get off the bus and go home. My throat was burning, and my breath made a strange knocking sound. But the thought of everything that was waiting for me at Sitt Souad's house gave me patience.

On the way to the second checkpoint, I saw a tank for the first time, rolling down the street. People were carrying on with their lives as though it were normal. I remembered the last time I had been beyond the alley's limits, in July about two years before. I had gone with my mother to Souk Al-Tanabal in Sha'alan in the middle of Damascus, which they used to call the Lazy Folk's Market. We went to pick up the vegetables my mother would prepare for the market to sell, and which covered my brother's expenses at university. We would dig holes in the aubergines and courgettes, remove the eyes from the potatoes, and chop the parsley and carrots, and it took a long time to do. It was all done at home. I tried to do as much as I could before my mother returned from working at the school. I washed the vegetables and the herbs thoroughly and got rid of every bit of dirt and every insect and little snail clinging to the creases of the green leaves. I peeled and chopped them, but I left it to my mother to scoop the hearts out from the courgettes and aubergines because I didn't like the holes, they were really ugly. Chopping parsley was my favourite game. I turned it into something like dust. I chopped it until it dyed my fingers green, then I packed it into small plastic bags. I even prepared the peas. I shelled them, and ate a few of them, and hid some of them—I would make bracelets out of these ones, and paint them my favourite red.

Once, my mother discovered a worm coming out from under the wooden boxes I had piled at the corner of the bed. When she rummaged through the odds and ends inside, I saw that my bracelets had turned into rotten black pellets with worms inside. My mother hit me then. She had never done it before, but when she did, she carried on hitting me until I blacked out, and she burst out crying and cursed her bad fortune and difficult life.

A young man a little older than me would bring the vegetables to our house. The checkpoints had increased after our visit that summer, so the grocer had asked my mother to stay at home—he would bring the vegetables to her and pick them up after we had prepared them. This is when I met that boy. He was the one who brought the vegetables and took them away again. I was forbidden to talk to strangers. My mother would tell them that I was crazy! This is another story I will tell you, I mean the story of the young man whose name I didn't know, but not now. I meant to tell you the story of the checkpoint, but then I remembered the first time and the last time I saw a checkpoint, and then I suddenly remembered the vivid colours of the vegetables I used to play with by making shapes out of their peels, and so I got distracted from the original story.

Don't worry, I won't hide anything from you. I will tell you everything I can while I am here in the cellar watching the end of summer out of the window.

The checkpoint I had seen two years before, the first one I ever saw, was strange. We needed to cross two checkpoints in order to reach Sha'alan to collect the vegetables from the market. The checkpoint was made up of a group of military-looking men and behind them there was a large green bus filled with soldiers. One of them pointed at me laughing and I stared back at him cheerfully, then he winked at me. When he did this, another soldier slapped him on the head reprovingly. I laughed, but the white cars and the men who carried guns and blocked the road were frightening. I didn't notice any sandbags back then, although they are scattered everywhere now, and there were no tanks. There were only men pointing their guns at the buses and passersby and searching them. I wasn't afraid, because there was no need to be, apart from the gun barrels, which made me shiver. So I already knew what "checkpoint" meant when my mother kept arriving home late and repeating that she had been held up at the Al-Jisr Al-Abyad checkpoint, then again at the Rukneddine checkpoint ...

I didn't know that the checkpoints had begun to take so many different shapes and forms until the second and last time I left my house, where the young man brought muddy vegetables and came back to collect them when they were clean, chopped, and colourful, and where I waited eagerly for his visits. I can remember the clear colour of his eyes, and he used to say to me that he knew I wasn't mad like everyone said, making me laugh. Then he would unload the large bag of vegetables, and I would help him, and we would brush against each other, and he would put his hand on my chest, and I would let him. The rope was long enough for me to touch him. My mother left the window open so the vegetables could be unloaded.

The young man disappeared and we no longer set eyes on him. My mother decided this suddenly, then she threw out the lipstick she used to wear years before, which had become a small piece of putty lying neglected in a drawer. My mother discovered that I used it (although it tasted bitter and left grains on my lips) when she returned early from work one day and found I had put it on my lips and combed my hair. I haven't told you that my hair is long, the colour of honey when it is mixed with wax. That day, back when my hair was honey coloured, I had put on one of my mother's colourful dresses. It was green with yellow and white flowers like daisies. I was thinking how I could be a garden, and it was also the first and last time I had worn a dress with daisies on it. So the day my mother came back from work earlier than usual, she found me cutting the parsley and making circles and triangles from its scattered fragments, and the large bag was placed in the middle of the room and the vegetables were all around it. I didn't raise my head to look at her. She spat and sighed, then she squatted on her heels next to me. She took hold of me, dragged my chin up roughly and looked at me with terrified eyes. She looked at me for a few minutes, then she stood up, just as quietly. Nothing happened, but the lipstick disappeared, and I found the dress I had worn ripped up in a heap on the window ledge. Then the young man disappeared, and my mother began to bring the bags of vegetables and carry them away again, and my brother started coming home early.

All of this happened quickly, and I forgot the young man after a few days. Then my mother brought home some woollen jumpers and said we had to turn them into cushions. Then she decided that I shouldn't watch television when she was away. This was two years ago, and I kept silent and didn't go near the television while she was at work. When she came back, she let me watch dubbed Turkish serials with her. She would shell sunflower seeds and the sound of it rattled in my head, but I didn't complain. It wasn't that important, except for the headaches I got from the sound of the cracking seeds.

I used to reread books I had memorised, because the shapes of the letters confused me. I wouldn't have remembered what happened if I wasn't trying to explain the story to you. I avoided looking my mother in the eye after the incident that had made the boy disappear. I never left the house. My mother was happy that I stayed indoors and my brother was also content and reassured.

The visit to Sitt Souad's house was the first time I had seen the outside world in two years. My mother was tense and I couldn't understand why she was continually angry. When we went outside, she gripped me, afraid, and as she walked she looked closely all around her. I followed behind her like a sleepwalker. The night before, my mother hadn't been able to sleep because of the aeroplanes roaring and the bombs thundering. The sounds woke me too but I went back to sleep, and when another bomb fell and I woke up again, I would find her sitting up in bed, wide-eyed. I could see her pupils staring fixedly in the moonlight. My mother was withering day by day; I could see the bones in her cheeks, and the small hairs above her lip had become a black moustache. She had started smoking sometimes. It smelled horrible, and she coughed at night. Our life had changed and I didn't understand what had happened to my brother—he had started to go missing from our house.

I heard him fighting with my mother because he was leaving university. Their shouting got louder and louder, and once my mother slapped him and he disappeared for days. When he came back, he found my mother sick in bed. I had wet myself, and stayed soaked in it. My mother began smoking ravenously. All the pans we used to prepare food were left on the ground, where they were stored, and we spent two days without eating. Once, we woke up to a strange sound, like this: *Ssa, ssa, ssa, ssa* ... My mother discovered a large mouse in our room. I thought it was a rat! She opened the window and cleaned the house and she threw out the rubbish bags and the mountains of empty seed shells that had piled up next to the bed, then she returned to her natural state.

I can't remember for you how those two years passed. What happened at the checkpoint has made me lose my memories. Even the eyes of the young man, the one I let squeeze my chest, I can't really remember them any-more. I remember their gleam and their purity, but the colour I don't remember.

I am trying to concentrate so I can tell you my first story.

We were slowly getting closer to the last checkpoint in the white bus. On the right of us, on the other side of the highway, were four men wearing nice suits. They weren't carrying any weapons. At least, I couldn't see any weapons in their hands. But cars were stopping in front of them and next to them, and men were getting out of the cars slowly and carefully. One of the men in the nice suits would search the car. They didn't look anything like the men at the other check-points. They looked very smart. They wore big ties. Their hair was shiny, neat, and combed, like movie stars. The strange thing was they were so quiet, and the people around them were moving like robots. Only one of them was carrying a wireless radio. The man sitting behind us said they were from the Air Force Mukhabarat. I didn't know what this meant, but the tremor in the voices of the passengers made me afraid, despite the men's clean, bearded faces.

I was thinking that we had to do this whole journey if we wanted to spend the day at Sitt Souad's house, and we hadn't even got to Bab Tuma yet. And although the thundering of bombs (it was said they were dropped out of planes) was getting closer to us, I was happy because I was expecting presents and my portion of the books and colourful clothes and writing things that Sitt Souad had never failed to provide me with over the years: watercolours and colouring pencils and charcoal ... So many things were waiting for me! The little bookshelf by the side of my bed and the leather chair were also presents from her.

I was overwhelmed by Sitt Souad's presents. My mother said that she couldn't have children and that was why she was kindly, and if she had had children she wouldn't have been bothered with me. These words didn't mean anything to me. She said that Sitt Souad was going abroad and leaving the country just like lots of people had done already, and she had some things she wanted give to us. My mother said that Sitt Souad's husband would take us home in his car because there were so many things and I was buzzing and humming with joy. So what I saw on the long bus journey as we were going through the checkpoints didn't worry me, although my chest began to burn from the drops of sweat that were pouring off me. Even though I had squeezed my chest inside several shirts and I was wearing a blouse underneath to blur the outlines, it weighed heavily on me and jiggled. Have I told you that my chest is huge? It's so embarrassing. I was wearing my loose red shirt and I didn't like how I looked, because the shirt was wide and long, and my legs are short and skinny.

The bus stopped in front of the men at the checkpoint we would pass to get to Sitt Souad's house, but there wouldn't be many more checkpoints holding us up after this one; my mother said that as soon as we reached Bab Tuma, we would walk the rest of the way on foot. As soon as my mother had said *on foot*, I burst out laughing and the world around me changed. This was my lucky day—I would be walking!

The bus was still stopped when I needed to pee, and I didn't understand the meaning of the sweat dripping from every part of my body until I felt the pain in my bladder. Hot breathing surrounded me on all sides. We seemed to be floating on a sea of cars with a few humans springing up between. The passenger behind me puffed out hot, heavy breaths and my mother looked straight ahead; there was a car in front of us, and I didn't know what the bus passengers were trying to look at. They were muttering and huffing and two of them got out and lit cigarettes, so my mother glared at them. We had left the house three hours ago, and it seemed as if this journey had no end.

The driver said he was going to change jobs, he'd sell vegetables by the roadside instead. The passengers kept quiet.

There were two women, and one of them carried a baby who was crying all the time. I thought of how I too had once been a child and I had been left alone, and there hadn't been any ties on my wrists. That little baby was so lucky, while the world around it raced ahead! Even its crying was muffled, but it felt like it was attacking me. We heard the roaring of aeroplanes in the sky and the thunder of distant explosions, but the people didn't seem to notice. As for me, I was shaking, my feet had started to shake, and my mother looked at me, frightened. She put her arm around my shoulder and bent her head and whispered *Don't be afraid*. I wasn't afraid at all! But I was on the verge of wetting myself. Seeing how much I was sweating, the man sitting in front of me leaned over and gave me a tissue. My mother took it and wiped my face. The car in front of us was moving and the men at the checkpoint were searching it. I was glad that none of this meant anything to me, I didn't love or hate it. I didn't understand why I had to be what I am. I realised, then, that I didn't really want to leave our house. When the driver started to talk to one of the men at the checkpoint, I thought of how I didn't know who I was, I didn't have any feelings, everything that was happening to me now was because of my full bladder.

The checkpoint was guarded by five men. This time, two of them were in normal clothes. The second soldier was searching the bus and its passengers. He opened every woman's handbag, reached his hand in and moved it in a circle, then threw the bags back to them. He looked at the men more closely, then checked under the seats, and everyone was silent. We were all looking at him, and at the other man who walked around the bus and examined it with the same intensity. I glanced at the cement checkpoint stones between the cars on the other side, they were coloured black, white, and red. Checkpoints were scattered all over the streets of Damascus, especially around the big squares. Around Umayyad Square, above the checkpoint that had been painted in the colours of the national flag, sandbags, white and brown, made a wall in the empty space. In Al-Muhafaza Square there was a statue of

Yusuf Al-Azma that had been hit by a bomb and rebuilt. In one of the books that I got from the library, I read that this statue had been altered by the years.

The checkpoints that we saw cut the roads down the middle and turned into walls that divided the streets, medium-sized walls, made from sandbags, but what I liked most about these checkpoints, especially the checkpoints around Umayyad Square, were the wooden guard huts that were painted green and looked like doghouses in the stories I used to borrow from the library, and which were the size of a fist. I was able to keep three of them—Sitt Souad would restock the library sometimes and pay for it with her own money, and I would get the old stories to take home. Sometimes she even bought books for me, and five years ago she gave me a copy of the Qur'an. It had a red leather cover with gold leaf, and calligraphy embellished with the colour of honey. At that time, my life changed too, and I'll tell you this other story later on. But, at that moment, when we were at the checkpoint, I liked the green wooden hut that was only big enough for the soldier to stand inside. I thought it would be wonderful if me and my mother and my brother all lived there, in a small wooden house like that, but my dream of furnishing our little house was interrupted by the men searching the bus; it was white and small and in order to cram ourselves inside we needed to hunch over and bend our heads. I hadn't thought about it before, but seeing the soldier with his head scrunched against his chest to look under the seats made me think for the first time that we became something like an incomplete circle every time we got into these small white buses that filled the city's streets.

The checkpoint men didn't find whatever it was that had made them stop the bus, the same as the young man at the previous checkpoint. But the checkpoint man who had been scrutinising the ID card of the young man sitting in the seat behind me reached out and slapped him roughly. The young man hit his head against the metal, and then the soldier screamed as he looked at his ID: *Get off, hayawan!*

I stopped shaking and I forgot all about my bladder because as he was getting off the bus, the young man fell into my mother's arms and she didn't scream. She stayed silent while I took hold of his head, and he looked at me. His eyes were half white. Their pupils were hanging down to the left. He curled up and turned his gaze away. He was still able to move. Then the soldier's hand dragged him away and threw him onto the ground. We were all silent while this happened, even though I began to feel a hot stream gushing between my thighs and burning me, along with the beads of sweat that poured from my belly button all the way to the bottom of my pelvis. I was frozen. The soldier kicked the young man as he stood over him and pointed his gun and yelled at him: *From Joubar, you sonofabitch!*

Joubar is an area not very far from Abbassiy-yin Square, where there are tanks and check-points, and it is the area that the planes used to fly over. I didn't understand what was happening, all I knew was that Joubar was under siege from the army, bombs fell on it, evil people lived there, and I would die if I moved now. I wasn't afraid, I mean I didn't scream or cry. The hot stream trickled from under the seat and my mother noticed it, and that is when she shouted. Things happened quickly then. I was squeezing my legs together and trying to shrink my chest inside my blouse, my mother was clutching my hands, she was pulling the cord attached to my wrist but as she was doing that a hand dragged her away, or maybe more than one—I saw lots of hands. My head hit the seat in front and my mother slipped from my hands. Then she got off the bus and was bent over, and she would have been almost lying on the ground if she hadn't been caught and held by a man standing next to the four checkpoint men.

The rope was scratchy and hurt me, and I felt as though my hand was going to be ripped off as I was dragged behind her. They were pulling my mother. My arm pulled her from the other side. My mother was still holding tight to the rope but this wasn't enough to keep the tie around my wrist—I was suddenly freed! My mother's eyes watched me in alarm, but I was free.

The rope disappeared. The end of it was around my mother's wrist. Feet trod all over it.

I was sitting on the ground at first and I wasn't moving, but my mother screamed loudly and pointed at me. She wasn't saying anything anymore. They were looking at us bewildered, and one of them took hold of her; she was looking at me in terror while they began to search the young man from Joubar.

Can you think what happened? You can imagine it: my mother pleading with the soldier, who was checking whether she was on their wanted lists; and there I was at that same moment, freed from her; and the rest of the passengers were hurrying off the bus, ordered off by the men to be searched. Three soldiers gathered, joining from the opposite direction where the cement checkpoint was coloured like the flag. At that moment, my mother was on the other side of all these people, she was shouting, trying to reach her hand out to me through the crowd pressing in, and I was looking around stupidly, as I felt the hot stream gushing out all at once after having been gathered in my knickers.

Also at that moment, I started to walk.

I was really walking! I didn't turn around. I hear a scream and I am walking.

I am walking.

I am walking.

I always liked the idea of a long road that stopped me from seeing the small details in front of me. I could see a road I had to walk, waving at me from a long way away, a very long way away, and one of the soldiers was shouting at me to stop. But I couldn't go back. My legs were driving my steps forward under the impression there was nothing to block them, so I had to knock into men and women and follow where they led me.

Suddenly silence reigned after one of them fired a bullet in the air and yelled *STOP!*

I didn't stop. I saw people around me turning and looking strange and falling quiet. I didn't turn back, and I didn't hear any more noise. Just gunshots. There was a voice shouting at me to stop and the sound of panting, which I could tell was my mother, but I didn't stop.

When another shot echoed, the world seemed to stop moving, even the warm air that would move a little from time to time had stopped, and heads began to crane out of cars, urging me to go back. I didn't know what was happening behind me. My mother shouted my name.

I didn't hear what the men said because I couldn't make out their voices anymore, and I knew I was getting far away from them. I suddenly felt furious because they thought I was mad when all it was was that I didn't like moving my tongue, and I wouldn't even try. My tongue was still stuck somewhere in my throat. Just then, after my mother screamed my name, I wanted to kick the sandbags that appeared in front of me on both sides. But my feet wouldn't obey me and I kept walking and passing the cars, until I heard shouting again and cars screeching, and gunshots again, and I felt my mother's hand take mine, and there was a sharp sting in my right shoulder, and it turned into a burning cord of fire and I didn't understand why my mother's whole weight collapsed on me and why she threw herself on top of me, and I fell to the ground on the hot asphalt, and I couldn't move my body and I felt my mother's breathing as she hugged me. Her breathing was very strange. She panted and gasped and she squeezed me with her hands, but I couldn't see her face. Her breaths were in my ear, and I was almost dying, and if I had died then, nothing in this world would be any different. I would have liked to kick everything nearby if it hadn't been for the uproar all around, and I saw the dusty boots of the soldiers surround me, along with other shoes that all belonged to men, and just then I was watching the red line that had suddenly appeared from the left where my face was burning from the asphalt. It wasn't entirely red. Perhaps it was black. I don't know. But I saw people forming a circle around me and my mother, and the circle was clasping me, and I wanted to move my tongue because I couldn't hear her panting anymore, her body had grown heavier, and when two men came closer and picked up my mother, I didn't move my head to look at her face. A few grains of sand got into my mouth even though the sandbag checkpoint was far away, and when the owner of the boots that reached to his knees (they were gleaming boots) took hold of me and quickly picked me up, I was very light. I was floating. Just then, and only then, I really wanted to go to sleep.

There was a woman yelling, but it wasn't my mother. I wanted to look at her. I couldn't open my eyes. I was falling, tumbling, and the fall was wonderful. It was suddenly like being rocked to sleep, or it would have been if it hadn't been for the burning pain in my shoulder. I could feel the body of the man who was carrying me, and I could make out his heartbeat. He wasn't panting. But the sound of my mother's panting was still ringing in my ears ... then ... I fell asleep.

When I woke up, my mother had disappeared forever, and we had crossed the checkpoint.

I WOKE UP a few minutes ago.

This is how I found myself, lying down and tied with a rope. And I was thinking of adding to the empty white pages now, so I'm writing to you from the cellar, my new secret planet ...

I didn't ask the nurse I saw looking at me curiously how much time had passed (because as usual I didn't know how to move my tongue). I could make a picture of it all for you, or I could draw it in writing on the white sheets of paper.

I suppose that the white sheets, empty of words, might make you understand, but I am not capable of doing it. So the pages don't get lost, I am collecting them where the boxes of glue are, next to the packs of paper. When ten pages are finished they are glued together in the right-hand corner, and then I hide those ten pages under the bed. When the next ten pages are finished I will do the same thing. But I swear, when I opened my eyes that day and before I realised where I was, lying down and handcuffed, I saw the drawing that I had liked so much for a long time. It was a drawing of the snake swallowing the elephant in the book *The Little Prince*, my favourite book, which, as I've already told you, I know by heart—*did* I tell you that already?

I opened my eyes and all around me I saw several shapes of snakes—flying, swollen from the elephants inside them, just as Antoine de Saint-Exupéry drew them—and it frightened me. They were a sort of blue-green colour. The elephants, which you could see through the skin of the snakes, were grey. I won't hide from you that I drew lots of stories in the style of *The Little Prince* when I was nine years old, and they are still in our house.

My stories revolved around a zoo where the supervisor put a group of monkeys in with a lion and a lioness by mistake and forgot to separate them. There in the zoo, the animals decided that they had to do something similar. Clearly there were lots of games like this which the animals could play, but those are other stories, and not our story. I was just trying to remind you of the strange flying shapes I saw when I opened my eyes, which reminded me of the stories I had written.

I raised my head.

Light came in through the window and there weren't any sounds. There was a woman staring into my eyes. She was a nurse and she seemed to have been like that for a while, standing over my head, like a statue. My bed was next to a broad window and half of it was open, and the whole window was covered with a metal grille and looked over a large room full of patients. The nurse stirred and moved away from my head. She was wearing clean white clothes and lipstick. The colour was like the red lipstick my mother had thrown away. Red … red. After the nurse moved, the light came into my eyes (she had been standing in the middle of the line that separated the two sides of the window) and I could see the place I was in.

I tried to move my tongue but I couldn't. My left hand was still cuffed and my other hand was wrapped in a white bandage that reached the middle of my chest and covered my shoulder; I couldn't move my free hand. As soon as I tried to get up, I felt fire in my right shoulder. The other hand was bound with an iron bracelet without a chain. The cuff was placed over one of the bedposts. My shoulder hurt. I had been sleeping on the bed half naked. They had bound up half my chest along with my shoulder and I didn't understand what was going on and the aeroplanes and the flying shapes of snakes swallowing elephants all disappeared. The sharp smells cut through me. On my right was a small girl, who was asleep. Later on I found out she was unconscious. When the doctor came to treat her, her body was blue and she had two large rings around her eyes that were blue and red and black. A mixture of colours. Why do we have to define and separate colours?

The nurse came closer. She was like a little elephant. She looked in my eyes then spoke quickly, I looked back at her and didn't answer. A huge young man came, he was wearing a soldier's uniform. He glanced at me and told her that they had killed my mother by mistake, and they were waiting for my brother to come and take me away. Then he went over to the girl lying on the bed next to mine. He shook the bed and the girl moaned. She opened her eyes slowly, then closed them again. The nurse gave her a scornful glance before going out. I guessed it was early because the sky was still dark. The young girl was tied up like me, with an iron cuff. The bed was painted white but the paint was peeling off. Spots of rust were scattered over the grille. On the other side there was a chubby woman, and her hand was also handcuffed to the bed. I thought for an instant that I was dreaming, because we were all the same. Can you even imagine how happy I was at that moment? For an instant I was so happy to see those handcuffs! And the sentence that the young man had casually thrown out sounded in my ears, passing by like smoke curling through the room.

I looked between the beds, and the bodies of the women lying on them were like the letters of this sentence, but they were flying over my head, and I didn't feel any pressure weighing on me, as happened when I couldn't follow the flying black letters that stopped me from noticing the girl in the next bed who began to moan and move around in her bed. She had a beautiful face. Her groans were deep and sharp, like a knife screeching on glass. But she didn't open her eyes for me to know what was wrong with her, or so I could make signs to her with my eyes. My new iron handcuff was stopping me from being able to think.

A few minutes passed and the same nurse came back, the one with the bright red lips, pushing a bed that had another girl on it. She seemed half awake but her hand was fixed to the bed and wrapped in a bandage. Her right leg was also wrapped in a bandage up to her hip. Her eyes were not surrounded with coloured spots. The nurse stood between us. The man, who had put a gun on his side, stuffed it between his trousers and his shirt and pointed to my bed. He asked for the girl to be moved into the bed of the little mute. Actually I wasn't that little at all, but I was skinny. The nurse looked at my face but her stare had no meaning, then she told him that I was mad and her face spun toward me and before I could think about the letters that had disappeared from the ceiling, they had rolled the girl next to me onto my bed. It was only a small bed but they stuffed her in, then they handcuffed her to the other bedpost and she yelled and bit her lip. I looked at her while she did all that, and her face went red while her body collapsed onto the bed and I wanted to cry because her body had swallowed mine, and I couldn't do anything except bite my tongue. I felt her screams like an earthquake inside me, then the nurse and the men went out.

I turned my face away to the other side where the window looked out over the second room; the room contained men, so I looked away and closed my eyes in order to disappear. In the air, I drew the shapes of characters from *The Little Prince*, from the businessman to the flower that stirred the Prince's heart, to the snake and the lamplighter, and I really liked the planet that had one wall placed on it—that was my favourite place.

The girl snuffled and coughed, and she whispered something I couldn't hear. I was confused and craned my head, and the blood froze in my veins. She was whispering in my ear and crying, while the light was increasing, and suddenly the details of the room I was in appeared.

You can imagine what had happened to me! I had thought, when I fell asleep as the man carried me after my mother fell down and we crossed the checkpoint, that the sinking I had felt as I collapsed in the midday heat was me going into a forest that changed every now and then, like in *Alice in Wonderland*,

and this room was the forest. This is what happened—the light suddenly came on! And instead of the white rabbit, there was a nurse in white clothes.

I tried to clear my head so I wouldn't annoy the girl moaning next to me. When the nurse came back in the afternoon, she picked up the girl with the help of a man and they moved her the other way round so that her feet were next to my head and my feet reached to her chest. I had closed my eyes again so that the nurse wouldn't look at me and demand I talk, when I got a whiff of something rotten from the girl and saw her blue and swollen feet that had blood trickling out of them. I turned my face away and I didn't cry. I bit my tongue fiercely and felt saltiness seeping out of it.

After I closed my eyes I saw Sitt Souad calling me to come quickly. She was standing like she always did, in her black skirt and white shirt (I never saw her wear any other colours), her white shirt with the lace-edged collar, her curls of lightened, carefully arranged hair, and her delicate gold bracelets. She herself was standing in front of my eyes, and I was trying to squeeze them closed and listen to the voices of the nurse and the man. I couldn't understand what they were saying.

The smell coming off the girl was choking me, but I heard her calling me (I mean Sitt Souad), and whispering to me to sit next to the wide desk. My mother was watching us from a gap in the ceiling, then Sitt Souad stood up and closed the door, and the opening in the ceiling disappeared, and so did my mother, just like I always did in the school where I learned how to read and write for the first time with Sitt Souad. She would bring the assigned curriculum every year and teach it to me. She did that for several years. In fact, I was forbidden to study because of my condition, so the doctor instructed my mother to put me in Ibn Al-Nafees Hospital because he couldn't find an explanation for what was wrong with me. Sitt Souad would tie me to anything upright, such as the library's doorposts, apologising all the while, and my mother would urge her, pleading, not to ignore me, and to make sure the cord was well tied. This happened for years and the school library became part of me. More correctly, the library became my whole life.

The library was by the stairs that led to the second floor of the school; at the end of the corridor facing it was the staffroom. The library was a long way from the administrative office, which you had to reach through a long narrow corridor with classrooms distributed on either side. This smoothed the way for everyone to collude with my mother. The headmistress and her assistant would not have put up with what went on, but they never found out in all those years. If you knew what went on during that time, if you only knew how happy I was. As if I owned the world! I used to believe it the whole world. Was it really the world and nothing else? Why was the world always found somewhere else? The library was my own private planet, like the planet the Little Prince lived on, and it was one of my most important secret planets. I had many flowers, not just a single flower like the Little Prince, even though the room of the library itself wasn't that big. But its walls were filled with books. I loved their smell, a strange smell. A smell of pages … or maybe … I don't know what it is. But it was the smell of the library, and there was nothing like it. I can still smell it, even now. The books were covered or bound with brown paper. Inside each book there was a white page containing information. I loved hearing the names of the books in Sitt Souad's voice. The book number. The year of publication. I memorized the books one by one. I even memorized their different sizes. The leather-bound classics were placed right behind Sitt Souad's desk because she was responsible for looking after them and it was difficult to lose them that way.

On the third wall I didn't come across any new books. Every book was old. There were books of history and philosophy, and translated novels. The fourth wall was reserved for young children, and I suppose they were the stories for me, at that time. Have you already read them, perhaps? But I'm explaining to you how I saw Sitt Souad when I closed my eyes when the girl's feet were by my face, the girl they threw on my bed.

While you are reading these words, I am trying to get you to understand how I saw Sitt Souad as she was calling me. She was sitting in the middle of her desk. So, at that moment, when I saw her calling me and I was coming close to her, I saw the notebook she had used to start teaching me the alphabet, and then coloured ruled lines began to fly around in the air, and just then, when all I cared about was reaching her, the girl raised her leg and dropped it on my face, and we both started up off the bed in surprise. I screamed loudly and burst into tears. Don't ask why that happened, my yells came out in spite of myself, and the girl began to shake and apologise, but the nurse came in and two men came with her; one of them was wearing military clothes, he stayed by the door. The girl stammered with some difficulty that nothing had happened, her leg had fallen on my face by mistake and I wouldn't stop screaming. My nose was dripping blood and when I tasted its saltiness, I screamed even more. They asked me to stop screaming and I didn't, but a smack from the man in the normal clothes with the gun by his side knocked me out. I don't know what happened to the girl because I woke up in the middle of the day and she was in another bed, far away from me, fast asleep despite the dirt.

Normally I can breathe fine, but whenever I breathed in then, the pain made me feel like a sharp knife was cutting through my nose. I didn't know what had happened but I could taste dried blood on my lips. I didn't get up, I turned my body to face the window opposite me. The gap between the sides of the window seemed wider, and behind the window there were iron bars, and I knew from the conversations around me that we were in a hospital and its windows and doors were made of iron bars, and a bullet had gone through my shoulder, and I had had an operation, and because of this I wouldn't be able to move for a few days.

Night came and I drifted off and woke up, I didn't taste any food and I refused to eat.

They treated me better than the other girls—I think they were patients like me—and I was thinking of the moment that I would get out of the hospital, and I would be left to walk, and walk and walk, when everything that tied me would be broken. This alone was how I could bear the various different types of insects flying overhead, and the mosquitoes, and the disgusting smells, and the bedsheets that were pulled back, revealing ancient black leather underneath that scratched and stung my body.

The next day, I was drawing one of my secret planets inside me, with closed eyes. The last drawing in *The Little Prince*, the picture of the desert ... There was a star in the sky and it was yellow, and below it a curved line interrupted by another curved line just above it, creating a mound. This was the last drawing in the book, where the Prince disappears, and I was covering my eyes tight to finish the outlines and the dawn. I heard a sound coming from the next room; the girls were sleeping, and there was no other sound in the hospital. A strange silence. When a metal instrument crashed against the window it made a bang and two of the girls woke up, they started up frightened then bent their heads, and their eyes were half asleep and their hair was messy, one of them still had a white wrap over her head, then the silence came back, and they lay back down again. The sound came again, and I tried to peek at what was going on. You won't believe what I saw. A straight line, like a ruler made out of glittering crystal, that allowed me to see into the room. The thin iron grille that separated the two windows wouldn't let me see anything beyond the gap, but I could see sunlight falling into the other room in slanted rays.

I hadn't eaten for two days and I could hear rumbling from my stomach. The rumbles were quite loud, not like my faint stomach rumbles now, in the cellar. I turned my back to the other girls and stared at the window with the metal grille and felt lost, even though the planet of the Little Prince was all around me and I could see it clearly. I wanted to chant the Qur'an, but I was lost and I didn't understand anything that was going on. Why had my mother disappeared? Why was I here? Where was my brother? Why didn't they come for me? In other moments, I felt free. I would be alone at last and I would walk, and I would understand the end of all the walking and the movement of my feet, where my brain lived. I thought how I would keep walking, and perhaps on my long journey I would move my tongue again, and see wonderful things, and perhaps I would jump onto a strange, faraway planet.

I was trying to pull the filthy sheet under my feet and lay my body on as much of it as I could, getting ready for my next journey. That opening was directly opposite me, and you have to imagine an opening of my whole length in the window, it will make you see life as if it is shaped like an oddly shaped rectangle, like the snake that swallowed an elephant.

In front of me a young man's legs appeared. They weren't directly in front of me, but I could see them, I could see his thighs. It was the first time in my life I had seen a man's naked thighs. In the bed on the far side of him, there was a young man whose face was wrapped in a white bandage with a black cloth wound around his eyes cutting midway through his white, bandage-wrapped head, and I was looking at his hand. His hand was tied like mine with the same iron handcuff, and even though the rectangular gap in the window was very long, it wasn't more than a few inches high. I could see that the bed he was sitting on was black and made of leather, and it had no sheets. On the next bed there were two young men. They were lying down. I heard them groaning, and they were blindfolded as well. It wasn't possible to see anything more than that straight line, and I didn't intend to make anyone around me aware of what I was thinking. I didn't know what was in the rest of the room. The last bed belonged to an older man. His beard was long, and there was blood around his face.

I can't explain things to you as they really are. In fact, I think it's difficult to form relationships between words and real life. The smells around me, and most of them came from the room next door, were disgusting. I don't know another word apart from *disgusting*, and I don't think it's strong enough. But the smells were choking and I could hardly breathe.

The girl on the next bed, who was talking deliriously to herself, said *It smells of blood and rotting flesh!* I didn't believe her.

After a few minutes a din started up in the next room. The girls seemed to know what was happening. I heard deep sighs from them, and then the beatings started. There were four men. The girls said they were from the Mukhabarat, not the army. I couldn't see them clearly. I heard them cursing and heard a scream that tore the sky. My hands were around my middle. I closed my eyes and heard shouting and abuse as they arrested the wounded men. The patients' shouting was hoarse, and I couldn't do anything except move my tongue inside my mouth and try to make it go back into my throat—it was a game I used to love playing to find out

whether someone could swallow their tongue
—but this time I really began to swallow it,
and it hurt a lot. I heard the yelling of the
men who were beating the wounded patients
as they lay on their beds. I didn't dare open
my eyes at first, but I decided there was nothing wrong with knowing what was going on,
because they might do it to us, and I had to
be prepared.

The young man on the second bed was sitting and his head was between his knees. A
black strip of cloth was bound around his
eyes and on his back you could see the marks
of a past beating. His chest was wrapped in a
thick white bandage. I had a clear view of the
man who approached the patient's bed as I
watched; he was well dressed but a bit fat and
his moustache was thick and a reddish
colour. The owner of the red moustache hit
the wounded young man on his white bandage and shouted at him. The young man
didn't reply, he didn't show any reaction, so
the man with the red moustache hit him
from the right, and the young man fell over,
then resumed his position, bowed over with

his head by his feet, and when the man hit him from the left, the young man did the same thing again. The second wounded man to be arrested was bearded and there were some bloodstains on him, he was being hit in the stomach. This patient had a visible belly, his eyes opened wide, and there were no wounds on his body. His face was dyed with blood. He moaned, but softly.

You read these words now and you can imagine that what was happening was like falling from a cloud into a deep valley. And that is exactly how it was! I was sliding and sliding, and I was falling and I couldn't stop falling and the pit was endless. My eyes were rolling underneath the ceiling.

I noticed one of the wounded men raising first his head, then his body. He seemed like a skeleton. It seemed that he hadn't eaten for a long time. He had a beard and his eyes were hollow, and as soon as he tried to stand up, the man with the red moustache came and punched him in the head so he crashed into the metal bed. I saw that and didn't understand why the man was shaped in this way—as I told you already, I had never seen a naked man before, I didn't know anything about men's bodies apart from my brother's, but he hadn't been naked and only ever changed his clothes in the bathroom. Now, with the nakedness of all these men in front of me, I couldn't understand it! Was nakedness always this ugly? The scene was harder to bear than the bombs exploding close to our house, even harder than the times the headmistress came close to the library during her morning tour of the school, when Sitt Souad would rush out and greet her and start a long conversation with her. In those moments, my heart would pound because I knew I wasn't allowed to be there and that if the headmistress found out about me she would scold Sitt Souad, and maybe be angry at her, and maybe sack my mother. So, in those moments, which were repeated two or three times a year, I would tremble and wet myself, and when Sitt Souad came back in, she would wink at me. When I wrote to her on a scrap of white paper that I wanted to go home, she asked me to wait until the headmistress

went back to her office. And after I'd wet myself the second time, what would happen
was that as soon as the headmistress disappeared, Sitt Souad would untie me and run
with me to the student bathroom, and there,
while I inhaled various bodily smells, I
would understand why the headmistress de-
livered a continual rebuke to my mother for
not cleaning it very well. My mother would
cry whenever she heard her words, saying
that she scrubbed the floor and the porcelain
with every type of cleaning product. I will go
back to those moments, which were hell for
me, when I was waiting for the headmistress
and Sitt Souad. They were the most difficult
moments I had been through, but I wanted
to tell you that those minutes stopped meaning anything to me when I began to understand what fear really meant. Later on, I'll tell
you what hunger really is, but since I am trying to arrange the story for you, I'll leave
hunger out because hunger is like a triangle.
As for fear, it builds traps for you in your
body, and becomes part of your organs in
your belly; and it is the shape of a circle, with
no beginning and no end. Hunger stops at a

limit, because it ends with the end of the act of eating and is difficult to remember afterwards. But fear stays inside you like a circle that reaches from the feet to the heart, and its centre is the legs and it wraps around you and inside you and past you and behind you and it finishes in the bottom of the stomach. To me, fear seeps like a hot trickle of urine, but even that was denied me as I watched the men beating the wounded patients. They weren't completely wounded; they seemed a bit like the worn-out bodies of plastic dolls, moved by a spring wound by fear. My stomach was a circular hole that ended, as usual for me, in my bladder, and I began to contract, and they were swinging their fists into the wounds, and yelling and cursing. I opened my eyes a little more so I would understand—why were they shouting and cursing in such a strange way?

The next morning, the nurse said to one of the girls that her brother was in the second room, and that she and her brother would go back to prison and stay there till they rotted. The girl replied in a weak, inaudible voice, so the nurse with the strange cap responded that this was the punishment for treason and anyone who insulted or protested against the rule of the President. Then she rounded off her conversation with herself and cast a scrutinizing look over us. I looked around me and found it odd that someone would say those words. What did they mean?

I won't deny it; it irritates me when I don't understand what is said to me. I felt stupid and blind, and that everything happening around me was a mystery, but just then, while I was looking at the wounded men, I remembered my brother. Where was he? Did he know what had happened to me? Where was my mother? I thought this must be a game, perhaps, or something like that. It wasn't easy to picture my mother under the dust, and to forget that she tied my wrist to her hand. I couldn't rub my wrist like I usually did, because the iron handcuff was hard and it hurt me, and I wanted to move my tongue and explain to everyone that I wanted to go home, to my bed, to be exact, and I wanted my bed and my papers and my paints, and I didn't even want to go to Sitt Souad anymore—I had to leave here at once. I started to scream as I stared at the men through the window. They stopped moving and the nurse came in, and I screamed even more, then I saw unknown bodies all around me, and I was screaming and curling up in a ball, and it wasn't a scream but a strange muttering I could hear, and I bit into the edge of the bed that I was now sure had been upholstered in black leather. Its smell was ugly and its taste was sour, and I was biting it and screaming, and I wet myself, and all the while hands were holding on to me from every direction, and I got a slap on my face and I didn't open my eyes, not even to see what was going on around me, but these definitely weren't the men from the other room. I could hear screams from the wounded men despite the slaps that rained down on my face. Something hot stung me in my bottom, and I started to lose my strength, as if a hand were dragging me downwards, and I guessed this would be the end of the pit I was falling into, then I closed my eyes and slept.

My eyes were groping the path of the light. My head was heavy. I didn't open my eyes (my bottom burned painfully where they had injected me the day before) despite a whispering sound that rose beside me. *Sssssss ... Sssssss ...* Then silence fell. And the same sound came back: *Sssssss ... Sssssss ... Sssssss ...*

For a moment I believed I was under my bed, close to my mother, and I was coming out of a nightmare, but the sound woke me: *Sssssss ... Sssssss ... Are you okay?*

I managed to open my eyes. I turned my head and there was a girl on my bed. Her head was at the other end. Her swollen feet were by my head. Skinny body. No trace of blood or wound, and as for her head, it was totally shaved. I lifted my head. She was beautiful even though she was shaven. Soft white skin. Her eyes were wide and round, the strangest eyes I had ever seen in my life. I was definitely dreaming! The girl was like a bald doll. There was a black ribbon wrapped around her neck; she told me later it was a lock of her hair that she had been forced to shave because so much of it fell out in prison. I stared at her. She smiled and whispered *Don't be afraid ... What branch did you come from?* She curled up and motioned me to do like her so that our eyes would meet, and it was difficult. Both of us persisted in turning into a semicircle so our eyes would meet. Neither of us could lift our heads for more than a minute—the nurse and the two men standing at the door and the soldier who walked up and down the corridor, they wouldn't have allowed us to. We would get a slap from one of them if we did.

She whispered again: *I was in the Palestine branch. D'you know it? I was there four days.* I moved my head to make her understand that I heard her, though I didn't know what she meant by Palestine branch. She was stuttering and her lips were trembling. *Should I be afraid of you?* she added. I shook my head and a small moan came from me as I lifted my finger and mimed no. You can't imagine how I did this, my finger moving right and left like a dancer. And she went on with her conversation: *Are you mute?* I nodded yes. And I didn't know why I did that. I wasn't mute, I could recite the Qur'an, but I had no wish to speak. And I loved reading *The Little Prince* out loud when my mother and brother were out of the house. How could I tell her that I had never found any need to move my tongue? That was all it was. Even so, I answered with a nod that I was mute. She was silent and her face became sad. Her eyes were grave. The little light that allowed me to see her features made her seem even more strange. She was wearing jeans and a black cotton shirt. Her clothes seemed dirty, and there were traces of blue lines on her forearms, and there was a blue spot at the top of her chest as well. She hid it with her fingers and turned her back to me, then curled into a ball.

The other girls murmured and whispered. The bald girl continued to moan.

There were seven of us, but only four beds. A small ray of sunshine entered and pierced the room. Through it, I saw specks of dust that were rays of sunshine before. When I raised my head for a few seconds, I noticed that behind the window some tree branches were swaying gently. There was a clear blue sky. I heard a racket outside. And so I pushed the girl, and she looked at me pityingly, and I pointed to the window, and she sat up like she had been stung. When she looked at the window, she said *What?* I pointed to the sunshine and the dust. She smiled weakly and lay her head back down on the bed. She went to sleep without a pillow. Her bald head was on the leather of the bed. As for me, they had put a pillow under my head.

The other beds were without pillows. She said *Did they break your ribs?* as she pointed to the bandage wrapped around my shoulder and chest, and I waved my finger at her, like this! Do you know how? I made the sign of a gun for her with my fingers, and two fingers on my shoulder in the shape of a closed pair of scissors. And she gasped *Where?* I didn't reply. She was trying to close her eyes and I couldn't understand why she was here with us. She didn't seem to suffer from anything that needed a visit to the hospital, and through the soft rays of sunlight reflected onto her, I could see a serenity that made her face look like it belonged to a child of just a few years old. It seemed very confusing to me. Because her body was like a grown-up woman's, and was very beautiful despite the bruises. Then she began to turn her neck and move her head, and I could hear the cracking sound her bones made as she tried to twist her body in several directions, and she told me that they had arrested her at the Rukneddine checkpoint. She didn't expect a reply, she was speaking to herself and looking into my eyes, and she kept whispering. She begged me not to let them give me any injections, because then I wouldn't know what they would do to me in my sleep! So I motioned to her with my head, asking her to go on, and from time to time I would try and turn my head away from her as she was speaking, so they wouldn't see us whispering together. They had already slapped two girls in the opposite bed when they were caught talking. When that had happened I turned my head to the window that looked over the men's room. Through the oblong gap in the window I saw a new patient. His leg was connected to the ceiling with a long white rope that raised it high, and the white bandage covered up his body to the hip. The young man was naked and skinny and wearing red underwear. I turned my head and curled back up around the girl's feet. She was talking about the extra days she would spend here, but she couldn't make me understand, then she said they had tracked her and watched what she did, and listened in on her conversations, and that she had protested and taken medicines to the wounded, and she had confessed to it all and she wasn't afraid.

She curled up until she was almost a ball and she said to me, *I think I'm going to die.* Then she unrolled her body and moved away from me and closed her eyes. Her baldness made her stand out, and the symmetrical shape of her skull showed, so that the curves of her head and her eyes mirrored each other. She kept quiet until the next morning, then she whispered to me before the nurse and the two men came: *Stay awake!*

She was silent when they came in, and they made her stand up from the bed with a quick gesture. She could barely walk. I was surprised that she seemed utterly wrecked, and one of the men was forced to carry her. She seemed to be very light as she went out and disappeared from my sight. She was staring at me. Her eyes were open as wide as they could go and she waved at me not to do anything. She raised her eyebrows, and widened her eyes, and quickly made the same movement again.

The bald girl with the wide eyes disappeared.

THE BED WAS filled with blood and I didn't know where it had come from, or where the bald girl's wound had been, and I had forgotten to ask her name. As they were going out I wiped the blood with my fingers.

The girl had been bleeding and I hadn't noticed the large red blot that had soaked through her jeans. I didn't scream, I was afraid they would come and prick me with the needle the bald girl had spoken about, but it didn't matter because an hour later my brother was there in the hospital to take me away.

When my brother appeared in the doorway, the nurses came in with a man and they unfastened my cuff and took hold of my hands.

My brother stood there without showing any expression or feeling. He pulled me away after all the procedures for my discharge were finished. He took me by the hand and tied my right wrist, using the same rope my mother normally used, then he tied it to his left hand. He said, and these were the only words before we got into a taxi: *Alhamdu lil-lah, you are safe, ikhti*. He wouldn't look me in the eye.

His face was like stone and the rancid smell of the leather bed was still in my nose.

I can tell you now how the story went after that, in my own way, as if playing with a kind of fairy ball. As if, inside it, there are tiny pieces of broken mirror, and I throw the fairy ball, catch it with my fingers, and gnash my teeth. Then I hurl the fairy ball on the ground, and it shatters there, and the little mirrors start moving within a blue stream (the mirrors are supposed to be silver). I mean, the blue stream will move the little bits of mirror, which will reflect the huge, blazing flames.

I can tell you the events as they happen inside the fairy ball, without letting you see that I am playing with it now, passing the time waiting for Hassan to come back. It is right next to me. The pretend ball is in the cellar heaped up with packs of paper and the remains of printing machinery, where I've started writing stories for you, and I am supposed to be telling you how the taxi took us away from the shrieking ambulance sirens and the hospital that was treating people, and I am supposed to be describing the corridors we went through to get out of the hospital, and how my brother was holding my hand tight even though he had done the same thing my mother usually did and tied my wrist so tight it hurt, and how I didn't dare to even breathe any differently than normal. My shoulder was hurting, and I didn't know what I had to do. I wanted to go back home, to my bed.

I am supposed to tell you, according to the movement of the mirrors in that very moment, that my head was thinking of the bald girl and her wide eyes and the blood on the leather bed, and was guessing what would happen to her. And where the two men took her. I could even tell you what happened to her. But this is not taking place at the moment, because the shape of her large, wide, tortured, rigid eyes hasn't yet left my head. It has remained, right up to the moment when I am writing to you from the heart of the siege.

How can I draw those eyes for you, like the Little Prince did when he drew the circle shape of his little planet? That is impossible now, because if I added all these drawings, you would need a much bigger piece of paper than this. It's a shame that all these piled-up pages are the same size, since I could have added different-sized pages into the pile, and stuck them in using the glue in the plastic box with a blue lid the same colour as this, the only pen. I would have drawn you some wide eyes, the eyes of the bald girl whose whites disappeared. Just as I can describe the roads that me and my brother travelled on after we left the prison hospital, and how the driver put a faded pink towel on his neck, wet through, perhaps because of the drops that poured from his forehead, and which he dried his fingers on from time to time, before opening the window and shouting a curse at the month of August. Perhaps I should talk about stopping at the checkpoints, but I suppose I told you about those at the beginning, and I don't want to repeat the same stories. Perhaps I can describe the sky through the iron window here in the cellar, where it shows like a pale-coloured drop of raw blue, and how I can watch the cats that pass beneath the abandoned windows opposite. Or I could describe to you how the broken buildings look. But I won't act like the fairy ball, and I won't turn this moment into a small mirror jumping inside it.

Now my mind is jumping, and I am trying to recall what happened. Don't forget that there are eyes inside the girl's baldness, staring at me perpetually, so I prefer to go on with my tale as it is.

I was always hiding under the bed in our house, and writing, but I wasn't very satisfied with it. I found colours and lines and shapes much more important than direct meanings. It helped that the bed was one of my secret planets, and I will tell you about that later on.

The bed is my friend. Firm, old, with tall bedposts, it was in fact another one of Sitt Souad's gifts. Its tall legs left a space between the bed and the ground, and my mother would use this space to stuff various pots and pans into, then over the bed she would put a cover made with sparkly thread (also a gift from Sitt Souad), and this was the golden bedspread, quite sheer. My mother would tie me with a long rope that let me move throughout the room, and when she was out, I would pull out all the pots and pans and pile them up in the corner. I would lie on my stomach and take out my pens and papers and write whatever I felt like, and would you believe me if I told you that I couldn't write without turning the golden cover into a curtain that separated me from the rest of the room? Then I would close up on myself like a square or a cardboard box and write my stories. After that, I would write down every characteristic and adjective of the things around me, and I would draw them in their different forms, because every adjective in language is a painting.

At night, after my mother and my brother came home, I would colour in these sketches. Unfortunately you won't see them, or I'm not really sure if you will have been able to see them, because they are still in my box, stuffed down between the corner of the room and the bed. But I am trying to make you notice my early talent at writing stories, which Sitt Souad used to praise. There wasn't a day that she didn't ask me about them. She would read the stories and then look at me in amazement and say *You're a genius, ya binti!* And that was as far as it went. I admit that I showed these pictures to the boy I let touch my chest and cling to me once ... maybe twice. The second time was very quick, but he held my face close to his while I was emptying a large bag of vegetables, and I thought it was important he know that I am not a usual sort of girl, so I stuck my pictures on the wall of the room. They were all of several girls in front of a river, and in each picture a movement of one of the girls would change. Above the drawing I would leave white space so I could write out the dialogue that went on between them (I had seen this done in the magazines Sitt Souad bought). And even though I went to great lengths to distribute the pictures, and I put the phrase *By Rima Salem Al-Mahdawy* on every picture, and I winked at him to make him notice it, he just looked at the pictures neutrally, then he went on staring at my large chest and said the phrase that he always said to me until the day he suddenly disappeared along with the lipstick—*Ya Allah, your eyes are so pretty*—although his eyes were fixed on my chest the whole time he said it. When he disappeared I lost all hope, and I stopped hanging the pictures up to display them. I hid them in the box that I hope I can get back one day, but now we will leave the colours of the fairy ball and we'll carry on from where we had got to in my story.

We were in the car, and I have already told you that my brother sat next to me in silence.

He wasn't looking at me, he was speaking to the taxi driver and directing him through the side streets, and even though the pain in my arm had started to burn, I kept silent and all I did was hold my brother's hand. I shook it and pointed my head to the window. There were groups of men bristling with weapons, gathering around some young men. My brother looked away, took hold of my face and turned it in the opposite direction. He said *Close your eyes. Don't open them until I tell you, alright?* His eyes were hard. I had never seen them that way before. His hair seemed to be soaked in oil, and he smelled disgusting.

I moved closer to him and gestured with my eyes to the side where the soldiers were gathering. Then he looked stern and put his finger on his lips, warning me. The eyes of the driver were watching us and he gave me a perplexed look. He said *What's the story, yabni? ... What's up with your sister? She doesn't seem to have anything wrong with her.*

She fell down some steps and hurt herself, my brother quickly replied.

The driver muttered something I couldn't hear and turned towards a narrow alley. His voice got more grumpy. *You'll have to get out here, I can't take you any further.*

My brother slammed the car door hard. His fingers were shaking as he grabbed hold of me just as hard and dragged me behind him. My arm was hurting but I didn't make a sound, and then we walked under the sun for a long time. We were walking and walking and we went into unfamiliar lanes then dusty roads where some trees were gathered. I wanted to cry. My shoulder was really hurting, and my brother didn't look at me once the whole time. He was pulling me and staring at the sky, and when he decided we should stop under some trees, he said *Sit.* So I sat, and out of his bag he took a plastic bag filled with medicines and he gave me a selection of tablets with a cup of water and said *Take them.* So I drank the water with the pills. I was looking at him curiously and I didn't give up looking, but he wouldn't look at me even for a second. He was smoking ferociously the whole time and making calls on the mobile phone that he had bought the year before, the very small kind.

I didn't know the type of tree with slender branches that swayed its leaves lazily over us as we sat. I hadn't seen these trees before. I reckoned we had been walking more than two hours from when we left the driver at the top of one of the lanes. We were a long way from our house now. I didn't know where I was, and I didn't have the ability to speak, and the pen I usually carried with my little notebook for when I wanted to say something wasn't here. My bag had stayed with my mother ... My mother was dead, so they said, and my bag had disappeared.

There were ten trees in the group around us, on the left side of a dusty road, far from the buildings, but close by there was a group of shops for mending cars. I supposed that we weren't too far from Damascus, but we seemed to be much further away from our house. The breeze had become suffocating because of the dust hanging in the air from the small trucks passing. It almost choked me. My face was burning from the sun and there was nothing for us to do but wait. My brother asked me to be quiet, but I kicked his foot and glared at him. He didn't reply and kept wandering around, examining the screen of his little phone and making his phone calls.

We stayed there for maybe half an hour then he said *You're a smart girl, do you get what's going on?* He spoke to me while looking at the sky. I stared at him, and moved my head rhythmically up and down.

My brother had changed a lot, he was no longer the same boy I had loved. He used to smile with his eyes before bursting out laughing and rolling around with me on the red plastic decorated mat. Now his eyes had become strange. What worried me the most were those eyes that I had started to notice in people I came across, from the eyes of the bald girl in the hospital, to the eyes of the men who hit the wounded prisoners, to the hard eyes of the passersby in the streets, and the taxi drivers—their eyes were all different now. I would have liked to draw a new picture of those eyes, but that wasn't possible because their eyes were taking on different shapes and I was imagining in my head how they were turning into wide circles. They weren't human eyes in my imaginings. They were sometimes square, or unnaturally rounded. They would take up the entire space of the page. Their whites were gleaming and they all had a black pupil, like how the eyes of the nurse and the bald girl and my brother appeared to me, and I was trying to understand what he wanted to say with his eyes that strangely widened, but I couldn't understand. I was quiet and hadn't caused him any problems, not now and not at any other time. He picked up a branch that had fallen on the ground and drew criss-cross lines and kept talking. There was an odd silence and a warm breeze and a sticky afternoon. We were on our own in the outskirts of the city, and behind us were vast spaces in which little groups of trees and a few houses appeared. In front of us were houses packed together on top of each other, far enough away for them to look like a silent picture. My brother stopped talking and untied my wrist, then retied it again, but gently, without pulling too hard. He was crying as he squeezed my wrist. His tears streamed down his cheeks and dripped onto my hand, the one he was tying, and his tears settled in my palm. I didn't dare look in his eyes. He whispered *Does it hurt?* Laughing, I shook my head. He looked away, and when he did that I just wanted him to look at me so he would know for sure that I wasn't sad and he didn't have to worry about me, but he didn't look and he carried on tying the cord gently, then he leaned his back on a tree and lit a cigarette, and he looked into the distance where the houses seemed like interlocking matchboxes, and the sky was completely blue and a propeller plane passed through it without any bombs exploding. We were lucky because we were in an area that wasn't targeted by planes, even though it was exposed, so my brother said.

I shuffled my body along and joined him. The tree trunk was very thin and wasn't big enough for us both to lean on together. He pulled away from me a little, and blew out the smoke from his cigarette. My brother wasn't like other brothers you might have come across, although I don't know a lot about them; I never saw brothers and sisters, with the exception of some of the neighbours. My brother was different. The most beautiful man you ever saw in your life. My mother used to say he was like my father who disappeared from our lives when I was just four years old, and we never heard anything about him ever again. My mother had run away with him one beautiful spring night, so she said, but he disappeared after a few years, leaving her with me and my brother, who grew up and swore and said bad things about him, and my mother was angry and said no one knew what happened, certainly death alone could have made him abandon us. These details aren't important, but they are enough to make me tell you about my brother, the most beautiful man in the world. How white his face was then! Even though acne had left scars on his forehead and cheeks, and his beard had grown, and unfamiliar creases outlined his features. I would say they were sharp lines, tracing his cheeks. Lines drawn very precisely. His nose was prominent and delicate and in the middle it had a slight curve like the drawings of Greek men I used to collect, but his nose wasn't as broad as theirs. It was sharp, and seemed arrogant somehow. The colour of his eyes was the same as mine. My mother used to say that we looked a lot alike, but I never noticed much similarity. That day under the little trees, I tried to learn his face more because I had forgotten my mother's. I tried to go back over the details of my life with her. Her face had disappeared. I remember the shape of her wrist, the one she used to tie the thick rope around. I remember the red colour left by the marks of that rope when we arrived home from the school and washed our hands and faces, and she would rub the places that had reddened. But her face had disappeared, and my brother was staring into the distance. He seemed like her, with a slight difference—his hair was matted and ruffled, and he wasn't giving up on his attempts to escape my eyes. She would never do that, she used to watch me constantly.

Now, I had taken on her role and I was watching my brother. Drops of sweat were trickling down his forehead. He didn't wipe them away. The hot breeze that was moving the slender tree branches increased the drops streaming over his face and forearms.

The heat was stifling. I picked up a handful of dust and began to sprinkle it in the air, but my brother coughed and took hold of my hand and squeezed it. I didn't release the rest of the dust. He squeezed harder and I didn't let it go. He squeezed and I didn't shout. I threw the dust in his face. It stuck there and turned into thin mud on his eyelashes and I stared at him. He said *Stop it!* without looking at me. He was crying. I didn't stop. I kept on throwing dust and he kept coughing, and I saw his tears gushing from his eyes and making white lines on his cheeks, and I didn't stop and I looked at the blazing disc of the sun in the sky until we heard a roar getting close to us. It wasn't loud, because it was from a bicycle with three wheels, the kind we used to call *tartira*—you must know them! Because I don't suppose that a man from space will be coming here and reading these pages, just as I suppose whoever will stumble across them will be a man—it's so rare that women wander around here, the military squads don't usually let them go out, that's what the women here say. But you yourself might be either a woman or a man. Also, it's not important, but generally women are forbidden from going around unless it's for something absolutely necessary and urgent, so I suppose you'll be a man and you'll come across these pages and next to them will be the single blue pen that my story will end with, and of course it won't run out before you know everything I want you to know.

Let's go back to the story so that you and I don't turn into splinters of broken mirror in the fairy ball and get all the facts mixed up. What I wanted to say was that at that moment, while I was throwing dust in the air and my brother was coughing, and the sun was coming through the dry branches and the green leaves that were turning yellow, a tartira stopped in front of us and my brother pulled me up, and I noticed a look in his eyes that I had never seen before, and which made him frightening. I trembled and turned my head the other way, because his eyes were unblinking, as if their spheres were made of iron.

Two men got down from the three-wheeled bike, one of them gave my brother a plastic bag and he emptied it at once. There were clothes inside, the same ones that I have with me now, and which I used during all my movements in coming to this cursed place, the same ones (some of them) that I threw in this cellar, where there are piles of paper and a window at eye level where I can see the legs of dogs and cats, and details of the pits the bombs have caused, and the rubble of the buildings that used to stop me from seeing the sky. There was a small piece of it, a small piece of sky the size of a long, narrow street. I will write about the sky street for you later, when I have finished off writing the story of my brother in the cellar, the cellar I didn't know I would be staying in when I was waiting with him under a few trees and the sun was burning.

Three men arrived who would take us through several labyrinths until night fell. From my brother I took some black clothes that I had to put on to cover my face and colourful clothes, since it seemed compulsory, and since these were the clothes the women generally wore here. The black colour depressed me and I couldn't understand what difference it made to be wearing black clothes or my own colourful hijab. He put his palm over my mouth, then I bit his finger and started laughing, and he was scowling and his head was swaying. As for me, I really felt as if my guts were going to come out through my mouth. We were jiggling on the tartira and my brother put his hand over my eyes, and I was laughing, but I didn't catch sight of his eyes. His brutal fingers enclosed my face and I felt like I was suffocating. The tartira stopped and we got down, and three ghosts appeared, faces covered despite the heat.

First ghost: *We need to walk for about an hour.*

Second ghost: *Don't say a word … There are tanks in front of us, and the other side is all checkpoints, I don't even want to hear you breathing.*

Third ghost: *Follow me, come on, let's walk straight ahead to the line of trees.*

Then we stopped talking. They were men; I couldn't make out their faces, but I liked what we were doing. We were like the sorceress and the ghosts in the stories. Each of them was wearing a white *aba* and a turban on their head, and they spoke with low voices and disappeared into the night, and we stuck close to them. My brother wasn't pulling me behind him anymore, he was holding my hand, and before we followed the ghost men he whispered this terrifying phrase in my ear: *One wrong move and you're dead. Don't scream, or we're all dead.*

A helicopter hovered overhead. I felt I really needed to move my tongue. The helicopter was a familiar sound, and we stopped under a pile of trees, me and my brother and the ghost men, and I didn't understand what was happening until later.

In the morning, I learned that we had been taking a road away from men who had a lot of weapons and were fighting, and that we, along with the ghosts, had been hiding under the trees. There was no movement from any of us, but I began to try and move my finger in my brother's tense palm that also seemed like it was made of iron. He pulled me towards him and hid me inside his chest. I was trying to see the shape of the three ghosts, and he put the fingers of his other hand on my face when he felt me fidgeting. We stayed piled up there for about an hour, then the ghost men decided to walk, so we followed them in silence, and my brother's fingers squeezed the hand that was tied to his. It hurt and something came out of my mouth—I don't know what. My brother later said that I'd screamed, but I don't know what it was that came out, because if I had kept my mouth closed, I would have died. When that thing came out and I heard it coming from my own tongue, everyone threw themselves to the ground and with a quick movement my brother pushed me down away from him, and my face fell into the dirt.

Maybe dawn was on the point of breaking. I could sense it from the dust, from the breezes surrounding me, and I let my mouth stay in the dirt. I froze. My heart stopped beating, but I didn't die. I found this strange. The whole world turned into a drumbeat in my ears. When I came back and heard the beats of my heart, my brother pulled off his shirt. It was light-coloured, and I realised he was wearing a striped shirt my mother had bought him in the Hariqa neighbourhood. It was his favourite, and I remembered how smart he had looked in it when he came to collect me from the hospital, and I wasn't used to seeing him like that, and I didn't know what had made him put on this shirt that was meant for special occasions (although it smelled horrible at that moment), but his shirt then became a wad that he put in my mouth. He made ties out of the sleeves and pulled them around my jaw after he pulled my head out of the dust, and he tied the sleeves tight at the back of my head. I noticed something shining on his cheeks. He rewrapped the shirt around my face, and nothing showed from it apart from my eyes after he had tightened my new hijab. I looked in his eyes and he turned his face away. He tied the shirt around my jaw then made me stand up. The three men stood up, and at that moment I heard light breathing and moved closer to him. I wanted to let him know that I was sorry because I hadn't done what he had said, but he didn't look at me, and my mouth was gagged with the shirt sleeves. We walked for an hour along several roads, and when the sky started to appear like a black cloth with silver holes mixed in, I stuck closer to my brother and the second ghost said *We're safe*.

Just then, my brother looked at me for the first time. It was a neutral look, like the look I sometimes saw in the eyes of the dead cats in our lane. As for me, I was underneath the sky decorated with silver holes, and I noticed a small, soft line dug into his cheek by his tears.

We had entered the siege.

A MONTH HAD passed from the beginning of that evil summer, maybe more.

We had entered the siege. What we called a siege.

I was missing my paints and my bed, and I tried to understand the new place we were living in. My brother and I were in a room. It wasn't small. It was part of a house where several families lived, in a place called Zamalka, which they said was to the east of Damascus. Even though I hadn't lived too far from here, I'd never heard this name before, it seemed I really didn't know anything about the world ... not even a semblance of it. And I had believed books had already told me everything!

Two families, who were very nice to me, brought me food, and I helped them clean the house. Each member of these families looked at me kindly yet indifferently, but watched me with fear when the planes went overhead and dropped bombs and I stayed standing where I was. Perhaps that was why they thought I was mad. I would stand under the plane and follow it, is what Um Saeed said to me. The strange thing is, I thought every one of them was an idiot when they were crawling like columns of ants, scurrying for cover under the plane's roar. Why were they doing that? They would have died anyway if the plane dropped a bomb on the area—only chance would save them! How could you escape dying if not by standing in front of it? Or at least looking straight at it? They were definitely mad! In order for me to describe to you what we lived through over the following ten days, before the summer sky rained those bubbles with the horrible smell, I would need a long time, and I don't think I have that time because, according to the number of threads I have pulled out of my black hijab and left hanging in a string, I left the bald girl twenty days ago, maybe more. That means I came to this place at the beginning of August. You have to know that I am precise, and I understand everything about numbers completely. If I had succeeded in speaking, I would have been a maths scholar for sure, my mother always said I was bright. But I refused to say a word, and honestly I regret that now, but it's too late to feel regret, or to train my tongue to speak.

I was convinced there were things happening, puzzling things that couldn't be justified. This place might be like the world that Alice went into when she found herself in Wonderland; I said that to you before. Actually, the world wasn't at all colourful like Wonderland was. The cats vanished and didn't reappear. The cats didn't speak, they just meowed and died and reproduced at an amazing pace, and their colours were usually pale greys. There was a white cat that circled the house—turning its white a dirty grey. It would meow in the afternoon as it wriggled and rolled under the tree in the house's courtyard. I mean the yard, my mother used to say courtyard and I liked the word. I imagine myself sitting in a courtyard and this pleases me, and I am very little, like a spoon tossed to the courtyard's edge.

When we reached the Zamalka house, Um Saeed said we were between Zamalka and another nearby village in Ghouta. I learned from what happened afterwards that this house saved us from dying. Our house was between Dweil'a and Mukhayyam Jaramana —I didn't know any other district in Ghouta. Once, I went with my mother to Arbin but that was a long time ago. The world seemed to be very, very big. Perhaps you don't understand my words because I'm writing without restraint and without sequence. Will you forgive me? I wasn't always a writer, even though I kept dozens of the stories that I wrote and illustrated and coloured inside my box, like I told you before. Do you know my box? My stomach has been cramping for two days. Thinking of my box and my bed can make my stomach cramp, and in order to explain to you what the cramps mean, I need to draw them for you like the beautiful drawings in *The Little Prince*, but that's not possible. I don't think I can draw unless I have a pencil and there are no pencils here. I will draw some things with this blue pen! But the cramps that remind me of my bed and my box (or it is my books and my box that bring on the cramps) are like a forest of lines crooked at right angles and interlocking in knots. Imagine that my stomach is a straight line broken at several points ... like that ... like that ... like that ... broken at sharp angles. The lines make living difficult.

In the Zamalka house, the glass in the windows was made out of clear plastic because the bombs and whatever else fell out of the sky destroyed everything. People swapped glass for clear plastic, and it didn't matter because the weather was hot and the windows had to be open. The door of our room, despite the stifling heat, had to stay closed. There were other houses apparently, but because those other houses contained women, the men of this house said they were a *harem*, so the men couldn't go inside them; although

I didn't know who the owner of this house was so, seeing as we were women and children, it should have applied to us too. The men came and went—they carried weapons, one of them carried a camera and a gun and he worked in the ambulances and everywhere else as well. This was Hassan, I will tell you his story later. It's a love story. Do you know what love is? Love also cramps my stomach. It starts on the left-hand side of the chest, where there is a fire skewer like my mother's knitting needle, a fire skewer that goes through your heart and comes to rest at the bottom of your stomach region, and it makes you stupid and paralysed. Love is a group of small planets with long thin arms dancing then lacing together into a knot of dazzling light. Love that turns all my muscles as mute as my tongue. But back then, I just used to sneak looks at him through the hole in the door. When the men sat in the courtyard and the door was shut, I would watch them. My brother used to sit with them too. Hassan (although I didn't know his name then) would go away then come back and, through the little hole, I focused my gaze on his face. Often, he was sitting right opposite the door. I didn't know whether it was accidental or a sign from him. He was my hero, and you will know his story later.

Are you a bit lost in this story?

In the room where I watched the men through the hole in the door there was a plastic mat and some large cushions, and they were sun-faded and clean. There were two thick blankets that turned into two beds for us (my brother and I would roll them out and sleep on them), along with a tap and a small gas cooker, three small glass cups for drinking tea, and a single small copper coffeepot. There were some nails in the wall. I counted five of them, thick, long nails for hanging clothes, and the colour of the room was pale green. The paint was peeling. As for my hands, which my mother used to tie to the bed, they were now tied to the window. The window had an iron handle shaped like chamomile flowers. My brother had inherited my mother's task of untying and retying. But he didn't tie me to his hand. He had started to carry a heavy weapon on his back, and he wouldn't let me leave the room. I would circle the room all the way up to the door. Um Saeed, the old woman who looked like the grandmothers in cartoons, came every hour to ask me if I needed to go to the bathroom, and in fact I always said that I did, so she stopped coming so often. She began to come every two hours, and I would signal to her that I wanted to go to the bathroom, and she would shout for another woman to come and help manage me. I was so happy when I crossed the hall and went into the bathroom. Sometimes I peed and sometimes I stayed looking out of the bathroom window until she shouted for me. Um Saeed discovered my trick early on. She asked me to knock on the door if I needed to go to the bathroom, because she was sick and the bombs never stopped falling and it was dangerous to keep moving like this between my room and the bathroom. But I was also surprised, because the bombs would fall on our heads just the same whether we were in our rooms or out of them, and when I looked confused, she laughed and said *Ya binti, you want to die and*

people to see you here, Allah yustur aleik, relax ...
After that she started coming and staying
with me for longer and longer.

She was lonely. Her husband had died in
detention and her sons were drafted into
the military regiments fighting against the
President. She said to me that her oldest
wanted revenge for his father who had died
in the President's jails. People here were
kind, and my brother was also kind, but he
cursed the President and I only wanted to go
home to my bed and my mother.

My brother was silent. I hadn't seen him
laugh since we left the bald girl.

I am trying to explain to you about the new
place that I lived in for ten days, maybe longer. It was the second strange place, after the
bald girl's hospital, and there will be a third
strange place, and that is the place I'm writing to you from, but in those days I was with
Um Saeed, and she was teaching me how to
behave when the bombs and the barrels fell
on us. After the first four days she left the

family she was staying with and stayed in our room to care for me, before the bomb fell on the courtyard. My brother came back to stay with me for the last four days before I left this place. I can't concentrate. I have honestly forgotten Um Saeed's face. She didn't look like my mother. She was old and she didn't talk much. She laughed constantly and made fun of herself and whoever was around her. She sang in a hushed voice to the women and children so the men wouldn't hear her, and she whispered jokes to the women and winked at them, and they laughed in response. In the morning, she would take care of me. She would bring a container filled with water and make me wash my face, and she would take me to the bathroom.

She changed my clothes several times and washed them. I was absolutely furious. I was used to doing this myself. My brother must have told her that I wasn't capable of looking after myself. Um Saeed would sing sadly. She had lots of wrinkles around her face. She didn't take off her hijab even when she was sleeping. She told me that we might die at any moment and we had to keep our modesty. When she talked about modesty, she would say *sitra* instead of *hashma*, and she would say *Allah yustur aleik* while looking at me sadly. When she said that, I imagined myself to be a glass container with a long, thin neck like the leg of a stork, and on top of the neck there was a stopper. This is how I imagined the sitra, and this stopper was the magic word that Um Saeed would repeat continually, while she watched the sky from the window and carried on knitting. She was preparing a jacket in red. She said that she would turn this wool, that one of the ladies had bought and offered to her, into a jacket for her son; it would be perfect for the siege, she said. She didn't ask about my family, unlike the women of the other families who would look at me like I was odd and try to ask me questions. When I didn't answer and kept staring at them, they were silent and retreated, and they began to watch my movements whenever I crossed the courtyard to pee. I began to feel a burning in my stomach and I didn't eat the food (there wasn't a lot of it), so Um Saeed began to make oil-and-za'atar sandwiches in the morning, and she would chop tomatoes as well. In the evening she would fry an egg with onion and tomato. I will go over what it was that made me content to be with Um Saeed with you, it's what I have been trying to tell you since I started talking about her, but I am losing the thoughts in my mind, and I am talking excessively. (So you know, I really love the word *excess*.)

The important thing I will tell you about the days I spent with Um Saeed is that the children of the other families used to gather around her. There were about seven of them. There were other children who would watch me curiously and make fun of the way I walked, but this didn't bother me. Of the seven children, the oldest was ten and the youngest was six, or so I understood from their talk. They seemed to look alike. They were very sweet, and they would bring three notebooks, and my carton of coloured pens, and four pencils.

They would take turns with the pens, and I drew lots of things for them that would never have occurred to you. For example, I redrew the Little Prince as he was pictured in de Saint-Exupéry's tale and I coloured his scarf in yellow, and that delighted them, and it astonished the residents of the house! Perhaps I forget to tell you that I really love the scarf that the Little Prince puts on in the story, because it appears to be upright and flying in the air, and it is the same colour as the prince's golden hair. The children would colour the drawings in very well, and I made them draw the prince themselves afterwards but they weren't any good at that. I added the ball, I mean the little planet the prince lived on. One of them told me it was the first time he had ever seen Earth so small, and I wrote on a scrap of paper: *This isn't Earth, it's another planet*. So he laughed and was happy and jumped around and said *That one is much better*. While this happened, the bombs started falling, so we all turned into balls curled up around each other and we left the drawings and the colours on the floor. The first time, when they curled up, Um Saeed hugged them all in her lap. I stayed at a distance watching them, because as you know I was convinced that turning into a ball and hiding beside the pillars would be no use at all. The next time, the second day, I rounded myself like them and we curled up next to the pillars inside the room, away from the window. It was a good game, because as soon as silence fell and the thunder of the bombs and the roar of the plane that hovered over our heads had gone, we would yell with joy, and I screamed along with them, and I know that something came from my tongue. Um Saeed would cry to herself but she didn't make a sound while she was watching us, and would you believe it if I told you they were some of the happiest days I have ever lived? What's more, it suddenly became clear to me that I want one thing in life, and that is to teach children how to draw, and for a while I discovered that I draw very well. I convey images of life as they really are, especially the illustrations in *The Little Prince* and the animals of *Kalila and Dimna*, and again I thought that my decision at four years old not to use my tongue ever again was the wrong one, because if I had been able to do that, I would have told them the stories too. Do you think it's too late?

It would hardly be dawn when the children started knocking at the door, carrying their notebooks and pens and colours. Their mothers would watch what we did while they tirelessly went on with their work. The one I loved the most, Aamer, was eight, skinny, never laughed, and would sprawl on the ground every few minutes, pretending to be dead. He would pass his time going between the dots that I made for them on the paper so they could practice drawing. Aamer, whose voice I only rarely heard during those days, drew characters from *Alice in Wonderland*, and the animals of *Kalila and Dimna*, but he refused to draw anything from *The Little Prince*. Um Saeed said he was an orphan more or less and that his uncle was raising him, but his uncle had gone to fight with the other men and so Aamer stayed with his cousins and their mother (she said *his uncle's wife*) as his own mother was in prison. I used to think, what was the difference between disappearing and dying? His mother was detained in the President's prisons because her husband was in the Free Army, his older brother was with a brigade of the Free Army. I didn't understand the merry-go-round that they would narrate about Aamer and the disappearance of his family, nor all these armies whose names suddenly popped up!

The important thing in all this is that in five days we were bombed four times, and the last time the bomb was on the house next to ours, and the drawing lessons finished early and the children all left in a state of shock except Aamer, who came up to me and said *Is it true that you're crazy?* I laughed and shook my head, and he replied *That's what I thought, no crazy person knows how to draw like that!*

That night, the bombing was nonstop all around us, but it began in the distance, buzzing. You won't believe this, but I can sing the Qur'an. I have memorised it, actually. I know it by heart from beginning to end. There were lots of mosques around us, my brother used to say when we still lived in our old house, and they had all been built in the last twenty years. I would go with him and the other children of the neighbourhood to an institute attached to one of the mosques. There were lots of children.

The girls were young, and I wasn't allowed to go in without putting a covering on my head, and my brother would tie me to him. The rope was long enough to allow him to wait outside the girls' room. The boys weren't allowed to sit with us. When I turned nine, they refused to have me, saying I was too old, and I didn't understand what they meant by that until the blood started coming out from between my legs a year later. But, there, I learned to write out and recite the Qur'an. The institute was small, and the person training us was a woman. The girls had other rooms, I mean the older female students. My mother refused to send me on my own, but this wasn't important because I was trained to sing the Qur'an, to recite it at home using *tartil*. The girls would cry while they were reciting the Qur'an in the institute, and I would cry too, although I didn't know why we were crying. I will admit that I was very afraid, especially when I knew that the punishment waiting for us after death was hell and the flaying of flesh, among other things, you must know about this? I used to wake up at night terrified by the image of a fire shaped like a huge giant eating me up. I couldn't sleep for days after that. My mother burned all my drawings where I imagined hell. I used to draw the fires in red, green, and blue. I put them in layers, and each layer was a different colour, and inside each layer people's heads were burning, and inside the heads I would write verses from the Qur'an that spoke about hell and hellfire. My mother burned them all, even the picture of the strand of hair we have to walk over! I would draw pictures of hell and hide them but they would find their way to her. She would burn them, and light incense for hours afterwards. She snapped my colouring pens and burned my fingers with matches. She said what I had done was haram and a sin, and so I stopped drawing hell.

Surah Yusuf was my favourite. I used to sing the Qur'an and I forgot the verses that spoke about hell. Once, I recited the Qur'an to the young man I let touch my chest, he was stunned, and after that a long time passed and I forgot about singing and reciting the Qur'an, until the day I astonished Um Saeed and everyone else around me in Zamalka.

You will understand that I don't have enough time to explain to you about forgetting. Later, you can throw away whatever pages you want to. What matters to me is Um Saeed who wanted to understand how I knew how to use tartil in reciting the Qur'an. Really, it was difficult to explain to her, because my tongue was stopped, and like Um Saeed I don't understand much of what surrounds me. Even so, it became a bad omen, because Um Saeed disappeared the morning after I recited. My mother used to know that I couldn't stop when I started chanting the Qur'an. She would sometimes ask me to recite certain verses but I just couldn't do what she asked, and when she heard me reciting out of nowhere, she would cry, and send up a prayer to God to cure me. But she never felt embarrassed in front of our neighbours. I forgot to tell you that the neighbours used to hover around our room and listen in on me, they did this ever since the day they heard me singing and reciting the Qur'an. They used to say that my voice would make stones weep. After they said that, they started to behave better to my mother.

That evening, after the boys left and Aamer asked me about being crazy, I started to recite. The women gathered in a circle, whispering and absorbed in their conversations. They were knitting and one of them, a skinny one, was shelling beans, and they were watching what I was doing with their children. It is strange how people suddenly appear here. They appear as groups squashed into tight spaces, as we were in that house, and then in other places they disappear and no one reappears, like here in this cellar.

When the bombing started and Um Saeed jumped to her feet and the women rushed out from the other rooms we looked like a large group spiralling round itself. Two of the men were there, and I opened the door of my room and Um Saeed was sitting barefoot, her legs stretched out on the doorstep of the house and she was putting a wet towel on them. I was standing by the window and trying to move my hands that were bound to the window, because I felt like the water pouring from under the rope was hurting me. It's true that the bombing hadn't stopped, but the sky was clear and a light was shining, perhaps from the moon, even though I couldn't see it. But it was the first day of the month, which means it was a new moon. There was a fire in the distance lighting up the sky. We got close to one another, Um Saeed and I, and curled up until we could hear each other breathing.

I HAVEN'T SEEN my face for a long time and I don't know what it looks like, and I miss my mirror at home.

The faces of the children around me made me shake. Dust surrounded us on every side, and water was limited. Their clothes were filthy. I watched their fingers on their notebooks, where they would leave marks on the white pages, grey dots and lines. Their fingers were skinny and hardly touched the paper, but even so the lines they drew were precise and fluid. They stayed like that for entire minutes until they were able to move from drawing one line to another line, so the golden scarf that belonged to the Little Prince became outlined like a triangle in the end. And the tails of the elephants in *Kalila and Dimna* were made up of half a round drop. I made them draw an elephant, an animal which appeared in both the story of the Little Prince and "The Tale of the Lark and the Elephant" (one of the first stories in *Kalila and Dimna*), and this was hard because we had to imagine both stories and two different drawings, as the elephants in *The Little Prince* were not the elephants of Bidpai the philosopher. Aamer found a clever solution, as he drew two overlapping balls and said that he had learned this in school before his school was destroyed by a bomb, and he taught the others how to draw an elephant too. I was absolutely amazed, because Aamer, of the mournful eyes and narrow frowning forehead, seemed to be a teacher by instinct. I missed him for a long time after we left that place. He used to behave like the men who came back from time to time loaded down with filth and blood and weapons on their shoulders before disappearing again. He used to say to me that he would go with them when he stopped being young, and that he wanted revenge for his family because they had been killed and none of them were left. I would listen closely to him, then motion for him to join the other children, and at that he would stick his tongue out and say *It's true, you really are crazy.* So I would open my eyes and turn my eyelids inside out and look at him, then I would imitate the evil sorceresses in the stories and he would jump up as soon as I did that and I found it very funny, but as soon as he heard me singing he ran back to me and almost jumped into my lap. The women started asking me to recite verses from the Qur'an to them when the bombing got bad, but I couldn't do that, and instead I would bend myself over and curl up into a ball along with them. We played at curling up like that a lot.

Once, in the middle of the night, the windows were closed and the heat was intense. Um Saeed had shut them a few days earlier when we woke up and lots of lizards were scattered all around us and all over the ceiling. This type of lizard we call a *jerboa*, it is small and the colour of a fair-skinned child with sunburn. They are harmless but the others were frightened of them. I gathered up all the lizards and threw them out of the window. Um Saeed told me I was some use after all and she tightened my hijab around my face, and that day I wanted to scream but I couldn't move my tongue because the hijab was too tight over my forehead, and I was sweating and needed to throw off my long clothes. The important thing was that I woke up and I was sweating a terrifying amount. My body was pouring water and I thought for a moment that I had gone and wet myself in my clothes again. I got up from my bed and opened the window and started to recite with tartil.

Um Saeed told me that I had to make the verses less musical. She said *It's haram to sing like that, don't put tunes in the Qur'an!* I didn't answer her—I don't know any other way of reciting the Qur'an. My mother taught me how to recite this way, using tartil. She would recite it like this all the time. Some lines of Surah Yusuf and Surah Maryam came to me. For years, my mother used to recite this surah to me before bed along with Surah Maryam (I mean Surah Yusuf), and it was very dear to her, particularly the two verses that I used to chant:

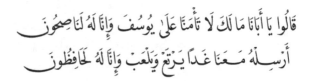

> On this they agreed; and thereupon they
> spoke thus to their father: "O our father!
> Wherefore wilt thou not trust us with Joseph,
> seeing that we are indeed his well-wishers?
> Let him go out with us tomorrow, that he
> may enjoy himself and play: and, verily,
> we shall guard him well!"

This was the section my mother used to sing to me, crying. I'm writing it out here with all the *tashkil* marks, which I find to be more important than the letters themselves. You can't understand what the melodies mean in these words if you don't know the rules of the music. I still wonder why tashkil marks don't turn into parts of the letters themselves? Why don't we draw them together with the letters and give them their required size? It would turn every word into a picture, like the pictures that are waiting for me in the leather-bound books of Sitt Souad. In fact, I hid those books in a safe place where no one will ever find them, in the bottom of my box—four huge leather-bound books of art history.

I will tell you about the first time I saw my mother in a dream, in the house in Zamalka. She was putting a hand on my forehead, just as Um Saeed did, and I woke up and she was putting her hand on my forehead and I saw myself in the dream waking up. It was a dream inside a dream, and I was walking in the dream and I didn't stop. I was walking and I didn't … stop, and I heard my mother's voice. Her face wasn't showing, I saw only her hair, and her fingers were on my head, and because my legs and my hands weren't obeying me I couldn't reach out my fingers to hers. My limbs were rushing forward and my body was ahead of them. I heard a whisper that told me to look up, and I looked up and couldn't see anything except a floating cloud, moving along. A single cloud, the size of my pillow, keeping up with me. I tried to move my head so the cloud would move off, but it just followed the tilt of my head and whispered that it would stay with me and protect me, and I was there inside it and underneath it and all I had to do was reach out my hand to touch my mother's fingers, but I couldn't. I knew in the dream that I was dreaming. The road in the first dream didn't have clear features. In the second dream I saw myself in, where I was dreaming that I was dreaming, the road was like the entrance to our alley—a long, narrow lane. There were no houses around it, just giant trees whose limbs wrapped around each other and stopped me from seeing the sky. As for the end of the lane, it was just a dot, and when I woke up from the first dream inside the other dream everything disappeared, and nothing remained except the cloud. I was trying to move my tongue and stop my legs from walking and my hands from swinging alternately with my legs, but I was unable to. My mother whispered *Look up*, and when I looked up, I woke up. Since that dream there has been a cloud over my head, I see it constantly. Now, awake, I can reach out and move it around my head. I touch my mother's fingers, and I smell her scent.

Opposite my window, where I watch even the movement of the hot wind in the afternoon, there are dust-coloured walls. Walls attached to houses. There are no trees there, just a burning sun. Maybe it's the desert. This must be the desert I've read about, maybe Syria is half desert. I remember reading that there's a large area of Syria that is desert but I wasn't convinced; I also read that there are lots of trees in Ghouta and this isn't true. I haven't seen lots of trees here. Maybe we weren't in Ghouta, even though my brother said we were. But that means we must be in Ghouta because he's never lied in his life, and so the story is here in Ghouta.

I don't know how I will finish this story because it all happened so quickly. It seems that while I am telling you these little stories, I am spinning round in intertwining circles, and every circle I go into has a new circle inside, and causes me to lose track of the previous one. All the things and events and everything that is happening and has happened in my life happens quickly. I think that this life is faster than it should be. To me, I am still in the time when I realised I couldn't stop walking, and it seems like yesterday, but in reality many years have passed—years and years. People don't have time to think about what happens to them. I think that they (and I am one of them) are like a herd of bulls, pushing and shoving each other while running and living, and they don't know what is going on, and neither do I. They are like rats, but the size of bulls! And I was like them. We wait, every day, for the bombs to fall on us.

Things when they fall from the sky seem different to how they actually are. The remnants of the bomb I saw were nothing more than metal fragments that didn't look like anything. When it fell from the plane it turned into a beast, and I couldn't understand how they could manufacture these things all at once just to throw them over these small, narrow houses which looked like old scribbles! Doesn't this matter to you? Because I have to arrange the story for you, just like I did with the story of the checkpoint and my mother's fall, and just like I did with the bald girl. Supposedly a story has a beginning and an end. But I already told you that we were curled up, and curled up so tight that we could hear each other breathing, so let's go back to the beginning.

The beginning was when the seven children came into my room. The husband of one of the women had asked if I could teach the little ones to memorise the Qur'an and write it out, since I was mute (he said). That irritated me because I had heard him saying this while I was watching them through the hole in the door. He was a fighter with a long beard. He issued his orders and for two days I had been writing out short verses for the children. I made them colour the writing in and turn the letters into pictures, because the verses began, like the women asked, with Surah Yusuf. I drew only Surah Yusuf for the children, and for two days we had been drawing the face of the prophet Yusuf, colouring it in, and writing the verse, and hiding what we were doing from the men. My brother still hadn't come back, he was also fighting. He carried a huge weapon. An old man said he was fine, and that I was to have faith in them, and that my brother was one of the brave heroes of the front line. I imagined what the lines were like, and this last thing I will tell you about later. The important thing is the story I have started, and which I must finish for you. So, as you know, we were in a house made up of several rooms with a courtyard in the middle, and inside the courtyard was a group of small flower beds. Stones were laid around the walls of the rooms, set by means of haphazard cement, and soil was put inside them, and they were planted with mint, onion, and other things. The colour of the soil was red. The red soil reflected the dark colour of the walls, but the plants and flowers were half yellow, and the women planted some mint and parsley in the middle of the yard. I didn't like the flowers. They looked a bit like tall, spindly trees that had been abandoned, and were nothing like the flowers I use to decorate my letters here. In the middle of the open space, there was a large tree, a white cedar, and underneath was a small table, extended so it could seat extra people, and the court-yard had lots of things scattered in it. Um Saeed said the things were piled here after the revolution began. Do you know what a revolution is? A revolution is what makes planes drop barrel bombs on us, that's what Aamer said, after the conversation that I will relate for you. You can imagine the children (who were in my room), and the women who were watching us worriedly and going on with their work and whispering incessantly. There were three families in the room that contained me and Um Saeed, and there was always a man sleeping in the house. The men took turns fighting and guarding the house. Um Saeed said that we had three women who were pregnant. One of them was screaming and pulling her own hair, then she came into the room crying, went up to Um Saeed, and grabbed her abaya. She pointed to a girl whose name was Rasha, who was beautiful and always very serious, and I had taught her how to draw the flower of the Little Prince, and her father had decided to put a covering on her head a few months earlier. The mother was hitting her stomach and crying, and whispering with Um Saeed and looking at Rasha and welling up with more tears. She shook her head with a swift movement. She bit her lip and from one moment to the next she pronounced a word, one word: *Child!* Um Saeed went right up to her and whispered some things we didn't hear, and then the pregnant woman jumped to her feet and furiously yelled the same word again. We didn't understand what was going on. The pregnant mother held Rasha over her stomach and was panting. She stared at the women, and told them she would run away with her daughter, that she wouldn't let him just do whatever he wanted with her. The women looked terrified by what she was saying, and they were trying to shut her up and pull Rasha out of her arms, whispering, so that the men wouldn't hear them, because if they heard, disaster would fall on her and on them too. Then one of the women got close to the pregnant woman and took Rasha and made her sit down. The pregnant mother was furious, and I felt my heart knocking when I heard one of the women say that her husband would kill her if he heard her utter this madness. Suddenly, one of the fighters came in, swinging a weapon in his hands. Silence fell. The women froze and looked down. The fighter man shouted at the pregnant woman and demanded she leave, and she went out behind him. She disappeared for some time and then came back. She was silent, and Rasha was still playing and drawing the face of the prophet Yusuf with me next to the flower of the Little Prince, and she was rewriting the two lines I had written out from the beginning of the verse. Rasha's face was strangely beautiful, and it is impossible to describe its colour. I tried to colour her face and it was hard. I used to switch between drawing the colour of her face and her mother's face. The colour of Rasha's face required a mixture of red and white, whereas her mother's face was a mixture of black and blue. When she was angry, soft red lines would mingle with it. Rasha ignored what was happening. She drew more faces with me while her mother kept muttering without anger, tears, or shouting. She kept glancing, frightened, at the door; Aamer told me later that the fighter who had come in was her husband. Aamer also told me that Rasha was the most beautiful girl in their neighbourhood, and she used to play with him. She would marry a fighter, he said, then he added that he was surprised her mother was angry, because Rasha was the daughter of a squadron leader, and she was going to be a fighter's wife, and this would protect her and give her pride and self-respect. Then he looked at me in silence. He continued looking into my eyes for a few minutes, and asked me if I understood what he was saying. I nodded to say yes. He was looking at Rasha's fingers as they moved, and at the colours moving with them over the white of the paper, then his tears came pouring out and he hid his head in his hands, and Um Saeed shouted at him and said he had become a man, and that Rasha wasn't a little girl anymore, and she was going to stop playing with him and the rest of the children, and he turned his face away from them all. He sat in the corner away from everyone, and beckoned me over to sit next to him and teach him how to draw.

The heat was stifling, and the silence when the mother stopped shouting seemed weird. I was touching my mother's fingers from time to time, and smiling, and miming that a breeze was going through my chest, and I would move my head and she moved with me, right and left, as I told you. The house we were in wasn't in Zamalka, it was on the edges really, closer to the open country, or so I understood later from the road we took to leave that place quick as a hurricane three days after all this had happened. Because I didn't know any of that at the time I started to organise the room as if I would be living there, and I tried to make a new box for myself.

The box I got hold of was a tin drum that Um Saeed said had a hole in it, and so it was no use for putting water in. I put it next to me, in the space between my head and the wall-side of the bed I slept on. I began putting the children's drawings inside, and the colours, and I kept them safe. The drum, which was about three feet tall and half as wide, I made into a kind of extra pillow for my bed on the floor, and I wedged it more and more between the wall and my pillow, then I covered it with some cloth.

I will return to the story, where we are still hearing the sound of each other's breathing as we cram in together. The women began to move after a few minutes, and they looked at the sky, and one of them said the plane had gone away, and the men shouted at us to get back to our places, but no one heard, and the sky began to appear in front of me again, and I breathed out. Our eyes were looking at the sky as if we were blind and searching for something, and it was no more than a few seconds before the open space that I called a courtyard turned into a pit, and we were flying through the air, and were suddenly crumpled under a pile of dirt and stone and glass from the windows. I passed out because a blaze bringing fire and dust and scattered things had made us fly. In those moments, as I was closing my eyes I saw them doing the same.

When we woke up we didn't know how much time had passed. The children and I were fine. I couldn't move beyond the length of rope tied to the window, because even though the wall facing the yard had been completely destroyed, the window bars were still in place. We didn't know what had happened. The number of men and women around had increased and I glanced at the courtyard. Bits of bodies were scattered all over, and I saw the body of Um Saeed. She had no feet and her messy hair was showing—her hair was short and completely white. Then Um Saeed disappeared and I fell into a deep sleep that I only woke up from when some fingers were brushing my forehead. I believed it was my mother but I saw the face of my brother sitting beside me. He was hugging his rifle, and his beard had gotten longer; he seemed like an old man. Before moving I looked out of the corner of my eye and saw that all the things in the room had been gathered up and the children had disappeared, and three men were finishing cleaning the place, and I wasn't in my room, and my box had disappeared, by which I mean my drum. In fact, we were in the back room of the house, which had been spared along with one other room where the only family with children that was left was crammed in. Um Saeed and two of the women had been killed. They had disappeared along with three children. As for my seven children, they were still fine, though Aamer's right leg had been cut off. My brother said to me, *Alhamdu lillah, you're safe*. He'd realised that I had opened my eyes, and I knew that my mother wasn't there.

I am telling you this story because after that happened I slept for two days, and on the third day, when I began to walk and could keep my balance and move within the area allowed by the new rope my brother had brought (which hurt), we moved to Douma. I mean, I moved to Douma, on my own. This is what I will tell you now, the story of the bubbles with the horrible smell.

My brother stayed with me in the room that had survived the bombing, and we were alone. The room was small.

The angry pregnant mother had flown through the air like the bomb and disappeared along with two of her children, and her daughter Rasha had stayed with her father. Our room was small and dusty and it needed cleaning. The explosion had turned it into a small hill of dust with its former owner's things crumpled beneath. I saw a high-heeled shoe belonging to the angry woman, its colour seemed to be a dusty pink but there were flower-shaped spots sparkling all over it. I know shoes like these used to be scattered densely throughout the shops in Dweil'a. It had been spoiled by a sticky substance, more than likely blood, yet it was sparkling in the middle of all the dust. My brother cleaned what he could and threw the odds and ends into the courtyard, which was now a pit. The door of the room was open and my brother had dressed me in new clothes. They were completely black. It was strange, I didn't know whose they were but they were definitely too long for me, so I started to mess around inside my clothes, as my mother used to say. The clothes were loose and cooling, and that cheered me up a bit.

But the pit and the sides of the pit were heaped all over with metal splinters that were strange; they looked like smashed toys.

My brother came inside the room and the children went out of the other room. They were touching the shrapnel that Hassan had photographed. I wished I could go outside and touch it too. I didn't dare ask my brother, but the children went out into the sunshine and played with the pieces. The silence weighed heavily and I was frightened. Silence brought painful things, or so I believed, and I understood now why Um Saeed had been afraid when the plane came. So this was what happened! Um Saeed had disappeared, just as my mother had disappeared, and I told myself this is what God wants. Everyone around me was repeating that phrase.

The boys made a train from pieces of the bomb shards but I didn't see Aamer with them. Just one woman kept moving between the rooms; she seemed grave. She had been with the women in the courtyard and hadn't been injured, which was odd, and she seemed to be asleep although she was standing and walking and moving around. My brother said he would find a family to look after me in a couple of days, and he wouldn't go back to the front lines until he was sure I was somewhere safe. I couldn't concentrate on what he was saying. I was dreaming. I saw a brief dream when I closed my eyes, though I was fully awake. I saw myself lying under the ground, with a slight layer of space separating me from the surface of the earth, and in the dream I saw plant roots that were winding around my neck, and my brother was trying to reach me.

If you had known my brother when he was young, you would understand what I mean. Back then, he was cheerful, he worked hard at school, and he was affectionate. He told me, the night before the disgusting bubbles fell, that his friends had been killed, and his (our) mother too, and that he didn't have anything left in this life except me. The whole Ghouta region was under siege from the army. There was no food and it was difficult, so my brother said, for the situation to go on like this, because people would starve to death. That last part he didn't say to me. I was listening in through the window while he was speaking with the men, and the men replied with vague and angry phrases so perhaps food was in short supply? I don't know! We could feel our stomachs rumbling between meals, which became a single meal a day: a za'atar sandwich. My brother said that the siege wouldn't last long, and that we would be saved and would go back home, and that I had to have faith in that. I would nod my head and look at him, begging. He came close to me and whispered to me not to recite the Qur'an again, and I wanted to say to him that I don't do it because I want to but I couldn't move my tongue, and for the first time ever I wanted to hug my brother tight so he would know how much I loved him, but he went out into the courtyard to help the other young men repair the house.

I fell asleep before I saw him again. In the next few hours, which I'm going to tell you about, I learned why I saw myself under the ground, lying down, and I learned that people here had been under siege for more than a year. The place was close to our house. My mother and I used to hear the roaring of the planes and the thunder of the bombs, and I used to think it was the rumbling of thunderstorms. Last summer, I learned the sounds were bombs, and my mother said to me that there was a war, and my brother said it wasn't a war, and as usual I didn't understand why they fought all the time. Now I understand. Here people are dying, and there they hear the sounds that people die from.

I HAVE NEVER touched a fish in my life, I don't know how scales feel but I do know different types of fish, and the heroes of stories and their sea-nymph heroines, and science books that explain in detail how fish are shaped. You must know that I don't know how they feel, not even how they smell when they are rotten, which people say is like the sea, and is also how the fish markets smell. We never went to a fish market, and I don't know if there even was one in Damascus, but I have drawn fish ever since I knew the colours. I will tell you why: because, most importantly, the outlines are easy to draw, and you can colour in every single scale and create an entire world of colours using fish.

One coloured fish equals all the colours of nature. I had taught the children over the previous days how to draw a very simple fish, and I thought what a shame it was that *The Little Prince* doesn't have any drawings of fish in it, but I had thought of drawing some pictures of a sea-nymph tale and turning it into a story. This was before the bomb dropped in the courtyard. I was thinking again about fish while my brother started to untie the knot of the rope reaching from me to him, and so I finished thinking about fish and thought of how the next day I would start the story of the sea nymph with whichever of the children still remained, by which I mean whichever of them hadn't been killed by the bomb. I wouldn't wait for Aamer to come back. They said that his other leg had been amputated, so I didn't expect him. I didn't tell you before but I find it difficult to write, I prefer drawing. I am not exaggerating when I say that I write long stories, actually I used to draw stories but here I don't find myself able to do that. I drew all the letters of the alphabet for you, and now you can enjoy this garden that is part of a huge forest. I want to finish drawing it but I am afraid that time is running out, and I don't have any colours apart from blue, and it would be really stupid of me to draw a whole forest only in blue. In addition to the other huge difficulties I have, I only have one blue pen, and it doesn't hold enough ink to fill up the white space with the necessary shadows. The thing I don't understand is how the colours are mixed here. Everything turns a strange colour, dirt colour, maybe another colour I don't know the name of. I don't know the name of the colour. I have never seen anything like it before. It seems to be a colour that takes everything and turns it into a strange sketch, as if the boundaries between the lumps of things were being erased. I can't explain it clearly, but I feel as if I am inside a big painting, and drain water is being poured all over it from the sewers that run through the lanes in our neighbourhood. You can imagine it. But it wasn't very cheerful, so I stopped thinking of the name of the colour that the bombs left behind them. I was on the brink of falling asleep—sleeping and waking, sleeping and waking—and the door was still open, and the remains of the bomb were still in the courtyard. I can't tell you much about the crowds of fish that were reproducing in my head, but they looked like planes. Fish were piling up over my head, and I was trying to touch their scales but I couldn't, then out from their stomachs smaller fish came, gushing over the houses, turning into flames. I shut my eyes then opened them. The drawings from *The Little Prince*, that I know by heart, aren't enough. I will draw that story I am still thinking about, and I will draw my dreams, but now I will finish one of my stories for you, although I don't know where to begin. There were lots of mosquitoes buzzing around my eyes and in my ears, flying between my neck and the pillow, and I couldn't shoo them away. We were still in the house that was bombed, and doors were being left open, I think two of the four doors were open, and one of them was ours. I wanted to run, to do any kind of movement. But I was lying down and dried up, and there was a roar of distant explosions. I wanted to look at what was around me, as it was rare that I could look at things properly, especially in the day when there were other people around. Now I was looking at a distant star, something shining high up in the sky, whose colour seemed somewhere between blue and orange. I waved at my brother and he stood up, afraid of the roaring of planes and the thunder of the powerful explosions. I pointed towards the star, and he was looking at me terrified, and I was standing next to him, holding his hand and pointing at that star, but the thunder of a new explosion sent us tumbling to the ground.

And, so, what I am trying to tell you is that this moment, when I stood and pointed at the star and my heart was pounding, was the last time I saw my brother's face and the gleam of his eyes. It was one of the few times I tried to recall the colour of human eyes, that is all eyes except for Hassan's eyes. I don't know how people's eyes are. I never looked at Sitt Souad that closely, and even with my mother it was only very rarely that I was absorbed in her eyes. I used to look at some spot that was far away from whoever was talking to me and surrounding me. But in that moment, when I was close to my brother and I threw myself on his chest and pointed at the star, and I saw his face under the light of a sky that was burning from the bombs, I saw his eyes and he was looking into mine. It was the first time we had looked at each other like that. I find it hard to explain to you but I realised what the eyes of others are like then, and I learned what fear is. He whispered to me, *Strange these lights, and strange these explosions.* Then he took hold of my wrist, which was connected to his wrist, and he trembled. He sat next to me on the bed that faced the pile of dust he had collected in the courtyard. He surrounded me with his arms and kissed the top of my head, and we fell asleep. I can't tell you how long we were dozing while we sat like that, maybe minutes ... maybe hours ... but then my brother jumped and I rolled behind him. We were like two depressed circles. Then we paused like two broken lines and there was a thunder of bombs, and I was tied to his wrist but I couldn't get up, and he stood and was looking angrily toward the window. I kept watch on the sky with him. We didn't tremble and we didn't say a word, and the bombs kept coming, one after another. The other families were curled around each other and we heard crying, and I sang Surah Yusuf, and there was no sound other than my voice. No one stopped me. They were quiet while I recited. I miss my voice when we heard the roar of the planes. You won't believe that I know how to make words and verses come out. I begin and I don't stop until I finish. My brother knew this, but he shouted *Be quiet.* And I wasn't, so he shouted again: *Be quiet!* And I wasn't quiet, and I went up to him and put my hand over his mouth, and I didn't stop reciting and he didn't stop shouting, then the roar of the plane came near.

The sky flamed up and we heard a strange sound, like the sound that had hidden Um Saeed and the two women and the children, and we felt the ground shake, and I fell to the ground and my brother fell, and I stopped my chanting.

Do you know why I am describing these details to you? I am just trying to remember my brother.

I think that I am still able to live, and maybe I will live, and maybe a long time will pass, and these details might go away just as others have. I am sure there is something like a long black lane in my mind, maybe under my skin, or even in my chest, because I don't understand yet how people can tell the meanings of things apart. The mind and the heart and the blood, they all shape the meanings of things around me. I will go back and tell you about the shadowy basement where my memories get lost (nothing like the hole in the ground in *Alice in Wonderland*), and where inside I get hold of lots of pages and I draw. Now, in the cellar where I am writing to you, I am trying to write the story of the bubbles by drawing letters. I will be optimistic and assume you will be able to solve this riddle of letters and drawings. The important thing is that just then, while the sky above us was coloured by the lights of the fires, we heard the roar of nearby planes, and a scream filled the place, and everyone went outside and ran. The sky became orange, red, yellow, and I ran with my brother. We couldn't split up because we were tied together, we ran without stopping, I don't know for how long. Four hours, maybe more, maybe less ... I don't know. We all went out together, and we started running and running until a group of men appeared and shouted at us to go back.

I was looking at where the bomb was blazing. It was on the side facing the town. It might have been Zamalka, or it might not. I didn't know which way we had gone. There was a man running and shouting like he was deranged: *Take the women back!* I stayed attached to my brother.

The men were getting ready to tend to the wounded, and my brother looked at me from time to time as we were running. I was wearing loose clothes and I had covered my head and body completely with a lightweight black coat, my shoes were Um Saeed's red plastic slippers. There were eucalyptus trees (which of course I loved), and the men were carrying torches in their hands as they looked at a building of several floors, covered by an enormous eucalyptus tree.

Trees like these used to come to me in my dreams all the time and dance around me. They were definitely eucalyptus trees, the same trees that were in the street of the school where my mother worked. I suddenly felt overflowing with happiness. The sky threw light on the green leaves, and I began to laugh (but very quietly) because the colours of the leaves were so beautiful, and I thought how I desperately wanted to draw every single leaf on the branches of this eucalyptus tree that reached up to the third floor of the building.

The men went to another street and I stayed with my brother and Hassan. They seemed to be close friends because they were whispering to each other the whole way. Hassan was looking at me while I was running behind them panting, and he had a rifle on his back. Hassan was a fighter like my brother and he also had a beard. He was younger than my brother; his beard was untrimmed. Sticking together, they started climbing the stairs of one of the buildings and a camera appeared in Hassan's hand. I began to have a headache, and I couldn't make out the shouting that came from every side, and at that moment the bombing started. There were people on the floors above, including Hassan, whose story I will tell you afterwards. I didn't know his name then. I had seen him before and sneaked looks at him through the hole in the door.

We climbed the building, which was made up of four floors. The staircase was cement and there was no paint and the doors were all closed. My brother and Hassan started breaking down doors and breaking the locks, and we found them all asleep, I mean dead, and I walked behind my brother and Hassan like a sleepwalker so that I didn't take in the details of the four homes we went inside. There were whole families dead. You wouldn't have said that they were dead because they were still in their beds as if they were sleeping. My brother and Hassan shook them roughly. A family of three boys and a man and a woman, and another family of five children and a woman.

The air was heavy. The lights and the eucalyptus leaves disappeared. There were points of light on their sleeping faces, and on the last floor there was a woman on the stairs. Hassan took a picture of her. My head rocked on the inside. The woman was on the stairs, in front of her doorstep, carrying a child. The woman had been going down the stairs and lay in a heap over several steps, she was holding her son's head, curling him up into her chest. Her head was raised to the sky and her mouth was open. Her face was blue, and I was trembling, and my brother took hold of me and looked at Hassan, then he said *Leave and take my sister … Take her and get her somewhere far away from here.*

Hassan was looking at him in shock and anger, and my brother replied *Do as I tell you.* Then my brother went down the stairs and I followed him so that he wouldn't drag me behind him with the rope. The doors were left open, all the doors they had broken down, and I was thinking about what had happened in order to draw a story about the doors, but I didn't notice what they were like so I can't describe them to you in detail. The doors were open, and we were going down the stairs at a run, and I was trying to close them, and there were lots of men who were going up and bringing the dead people down. I didn't know why I was trying to close the doors but my brother shouted at me to stop doing it and I was trying to close them again and I was only aware that my head was going to explode from pain, and I almost choked, and I couldn't see anymore but I was running, and we came into the street and the eucalyptus trees were behind us. On one of the corners, while I felt dizzy and my eyes strained open and something like thorns began scratching me, starting from my throat, my brother untied the rope from his wrist and tied it to Hassan's wrist, and Hassan was furious. He said *Let me stay with you all.* My brother got very close to him and said *Get her somewhere safe, and come back to us. You have to go to Arbin, got it?* They looked at each other for a few seconds then hugged each other. My brother came up to me and crushed me to his chest, and I was hurting but I didn't do anything, and my hands stayed limp and my head was moving strangely and my eyes were widened, and I didn't look at him as he squeezed me and inhaled me, and then he ran off.

All of this lasted no more than a few minutes.

I say it was like this because I can't remember it clearly anymore, and the smells were disgusting, and that is when I learned the planes and the sky rained smells in August.

Hassan ran and I followed him. He didn't turn around, and I didn't turn around to know where my brother had disappeared to. I ran behind Hassan and I didn't scream or stamp my feet as I did with my brother whenever he didn't obey me. I ran behind Hassan and I could hear him crying. The horrible smells got worse, and the explosions weren't stopping and there were running men going across and raising their hands to the sky shouting *I testify there is no god but God and I testify that Muhammad is His prophet.* Their eyes were popping out, I could see them even in the darkness. The sky was blazing. The ground turned around us. I can't describe life very precisely for you at that moment. I mean, were we alive or were we dead? Everything turned into moving pictures. I thought again that I was Alice in Wonderland, and that the Cheshire Cat might appear at any moment—maybe he was there already, over by the eucalyptus tree. It was the first time my brother and my mother had left me with a stranger. I tried to take the rope off my wrist while I was panting behind Hassan, and I bit the rope fiercely, and I bit my flesh, and I kept biting until I could taste the saltiness of my blood, but the rope didn't break. Hassan was turning and running, and he didn't look behind him, he was crying and carrying his weapon on his shoulder; I remember that it was in his right hand. I was running behind him and he was dragging me. I couldn't see anymore, I was choking, then I lost one of my red slippers but I didn't stop. One of my feet stayed barefoot and I didn't scream. I heard the sound of an ambulance then the ground fell away and I was flying and I saw a lump of fire. I don't know where I landed. There was a roar of planes and I thought it was dawn. I smelled an odd smell, not the stinging smell, and not the dust that my face fell on. Grains of dust went into my mouth. Hassan dragged me behind him after I fell, pulling my body over the dirt that was still going in my mouth and I couldn't get up and follow him. I closed my eyes. I thought I would wake up and this would all be a nightmare, and I would be in my bed, at home with my mother and my brother.

I couldn't close my mouth, my face felt paralysed and my mouth filled with dirt, and I couldn't breathe anymore, and the air that came in through my nose was horrible, and I felt drowsy and wanted to spit. I closed my eyes and thought that I would sleep, and before I dozed off I saw Hassan running and bending over me and taking the dirt out of my mouth (but I was sleeping), and I saw Hassan's face come close to mine, then he picked me up and shook the dirt out of my mouth and ran. I was sleeping.

The smell was horrible. My brother disappeared into it.

WHILE I WRITE these words to you, I feel like I'm in a better state. It isn't the state that I've been in throughout my life, but the state that distances me from what happened that night, and from what is happening now, while I am waiting for Hassan to come back.

Six days have passed and he hasn't come yet. There's no water here and, since the beginning of the siege, no electricity either. I haven't washed my face for three days. I am just writing to you. All I am doing is writing. I only stop at night, when there's no light. Luckily, days in the summer are long. Writing needs a lot of time because, as you know, my letters are drawings.

I felt red spots on my skin and I was sweating a lot because the cellar was crammed with bundles of paper. The open window brings dust and floating fragments of bombs. Even so, I feel much better, because I have strange beings here in this cellar with me. I am excellent at moving alongside them while my wrist is tied to the iron bar of a high window that I can't reach. Hassan tied it, and the rope is long enough for me to go to the toilet, but despite this I haven't been to the toilet in two days. There's no water, and I can feel a weird itch between my thighs and in the middle of my chest. When the red spots appeared, I scratched them day and night without realising I was doing it.

I will tell you what apparatus this cellar contains, but first I would like to go on telling you the whole story. I would like to draw it for you, but I am unable to and my throat is dry.

I was telling you that I fell asleep and Hassan was running with me. I thought I was in a dream, that I must be Alice. Although I still remember the moments while I was sleeping, they have become just sketches. I was watching the dust around us and the shape of the road that my head was dangling towards. The whole world had turned to dust. Hassan carried me like he was carrying a sack of potatoes. He made my head go down to the bottom of his back. I was flopping like a rag. And I was sick on the road (it wasn't exactly sick but something was coming out of my mouth), and noises came from every direction. These were just moments. Hassan told me that we were riding in a small truck and going towards the hospital. I didn't know where this hospital was but I woke up in it, or so I learned later on from Hassan, who used to give me strange looks. He never stopped staring at me, and I liked it and it made me happy.

I haven't described Hassan for you yet. I am still waiting for him. He was better looking than my brother. It was difficult to tell him how old I am when my tongue wouldn't move. He was thin; his features were delicate. His beard, which was growing longer, was sprinkled over his cheeks and he seemed proud of it as he moved his fingers over it constantly. His weapon seemed funny while he was carrying it—honestly, it seemed huge on him, but I saw him firing it several times. Hassan is brave, and his eyes were the first ones I saw when I opened my eyes in the hospital. I mean the place that was like a cage; I don't know what else it looks like. I will try to understand that place I woke up in, and where I saw those eyes. Hassan was looking at me affectionately, sprinkling water on my body. He was wrapping me in a cover and had taken some of my clothes off, and I heard a man shouting at him, saying *Haram aleik! That's sinful, respect her hurma*, and Hassan put a light cover on me, and I was soaked in water, my hair was soaked, and Hassan put a cover on my head and twisted my long hair around his fingers, and the man came up to him and said *Respect the hurma*, so Hassan yelled at him: *She's my sister!* Then he moved next to me, and there was a young man, they had taken some of his clothes off and he was only wearing his underwear. He was beautiful but his eyes were open and he wasn't blinking, and I still felt burning in my eyes, and stinging in my chest, and I wanted to throw up.

The room was large and bodies were lying on the ground. There were people shouting, shouting came from everywhere. And there were women wrapped in clothes with hijabs covering their heads, and Hassan was shouting at the man that he was the reason those women were dead. I didn't understand what this meant, but later on in the cellar Hassan would tell me the planes dropped bombs on us that had poison gas inside, and these gases can penetrate clothing, and if someone is affected you have to take off their clothes so they won't die. The women who had been treated had stayed in their clothes because the men said it was sinful for women to be uncovered in front of men, and Hassan was furious.

The young man's body was next to me and there were lots of bodies distributed all around me, and once again I thought I was in a dream, and I said this wasn't a dream but a nightmare, and my hands were released and the rope was untied. I was free. I could walk and run without stopping—but I wasn't able to get up. I tried to raise my head. Hassan was sprinkling water on the bodies of some young men who were shaking and moving their limbs oddly. There and then, my head rose an inch or so from the water-soaked floor and I had a good view of the place. Hassan turned to me and looked in my eyes, and I began to understand. We were in another hospital, not the hospital of the bald girl, and this hospital was unusual because people were lying on the ground in strange shapes, and men and women were running about and doing the necessary treatments as Hassan had said, and lying in front of me were the bodies of several children. They were wearing pyjamas. They were very young and their eyes were closed, and if it wasn't for the foam coming out of their noses and the orange-coloured streams coming out of their mouths and the blueness creeping over their bodies, you would have thought they were sleeping. But I knew they weren't sleeping, and that they would disappear just as my mother and others had disappeared. The colours around me weren't dark. They were lit up with death.

I felt a weird creature moving inside my bowels, as if something wanted to come out from inside me, and I couldn't breathe, until suddenly there was a strong hand taking hold of me and I felt a needle sting my hand, and I was falling. And now I will tell you the secret that made me believe I was in a dream at that moment. The secret is that in those moments only, in the prison hospital and there in the hospital in Arbin, I was like everyone else, and I thought I was dreaming that people were living like me. I was suddenly content. There was someone like me in this world, even if this world seemed like a nightmare. I relaxed, and I hit my head against the ground (this is what I have done in moments of anger all my life), and I could see others doing this in different ways. In fact, there was a man moving his leg to the left and the right and he was screaming and everyone around him was asking him to do something. They were shouting *Say the shahada, say the shahada: There is no god but God*, and the man was beating his leg. And there was a young girl moving her head and neck in a similar way to me, but it was hard to make out her movements. I looked at Hassan for a moment. I wanted him to stay next to me and take me and pick me up. I thought all this might be a dream or a nightmare, and I thought there were things in life that might happen to people, and these things were happening to me, and once again I wasn't different from other people, and this made me happier than ever. But later on, Hassan would tell me that this wasn't true.

Back then, when I was beating my head, he came to me and took my head and placed it in his lap and whispered *Don't die.*

He spoke in a whisper. If they had known he wasn't my brother they would have kept him away from me. This is what he told me afterwards, when we were in the cellar. It was sinful for him to be near a woman and to touch her. He took hold of my head and said I would be fine, I had to sleep now, and he would keep looking after me but he would go and come back, and he wouldn't tie my wrist with the rope as my brother had ordered, but I wouldn't be able to move. Then he came close to me. His eyes were the most beautiful eyes I have seen in my life. Hassan was looking at me with huge eyes, like the eyes of the princes in stories. His eyes were the colour of honey. He tilted my head between his hands. I had only been mildly affected, he said.

Don't look at me!

Maybe you are looking at me while I am writing. You are picturing me, how I write. You are imagining that what I write is a story. Throw those ideas away. Put your heart in your feet and throw it like a fairy ball. You will understand what I am saying. How I wish my feet would respond to my head. There is a gap in me that I have to speak about. It comes accompanied by pictures like drawings in water, and I understand events around me in this way ... as drawings like water. The original water. What we see and what we live are just drawings in water to me. Can you prove to me that it isn't so? Here, under the window of the cellar I'm writing to you from, where I put my head for the faint light because the candles have just run out and I am now forced to leave off writing at night. Night, which I'll tell you about later, where impressionist and non-impressionist life disappears.

Facing me now is a large destroyed building. Half of it has turned into a pile of rocks. A plane bombed it two days ago and the glass in this window went flying and sliced up the air. I am not afraid that cats and dogs will come in here, I am never afraid that a wild animal will leap inside, because there is an iron grille. But I am afraid of one thing, and I will explain it when I am finished with the watery pictures of the room in the hospital. In front of me, at the cellar window, a bike is going past quickly, and I can hardly concentrate on finishing the story. The young man on the bike is going fast and tilting to one side; my brother and I used to do that on his bike. He used to take me for rides. He had a bicycle, as I told you, and his was much more beautiful than the one that just went past. I thought of shouting to the boy and telling him I'm here, but then I thought that Hassan would be angry because he asked me to keep silent until he came back. Perhaps he is coming back tomorrow, and what if I had told the young man I am here? It's the first time I've seen anyone going along this street. I'm scared—if he comes back I'll shout to him. But my tongue doesn't obey me, how will I shout? Perhaps I should scream and knock on the window bars. I did that just now, even though Hassan ordered me to watch out and keep quiet because he would go away and come back for me. I don't know what is taking him so long.

I'll go back to my story. I was thinking, while I was lying on the floor in the hospital and Hassan was wiping my face with water, of two coloured lumps that were in front of me. Things blended into each other in my mind; the ground was soaked in water, and that made me feel like I was in a painting. They were spraying water over everyone. Women wearing white were moving between the lumps thrown on the ground. There was a group of naked men, and on the opposite side there was a group of women, fully dressed. The women were dead, they weren't moving. Some of the bodies of the men thrown on the floor were moving. Strange cries and shifting sounds and a crash. There were phantoms shimmering in front of me and my vision was blurred.

I believed at that moment that this was the world we have to pass through when we move between life and death. That is what I thought, and I was wondering why the scene didn't appear to be taking place on a cloud, or in a deep valley. If this was the place that would take me to my mother, then it had to be different, since here there were walls. At the end of the room or corridor (I realised that it resembled a corridor) there were also beds, and on the beds people were scream-ing. I didn't know whether they were men or women or children. The screams blended together, even though there was also the roar of planes. Hassan told me later that after dropping the gas, the planes would come back to drop bombs again and hit the ambulances that had come to rescue the injured and the people who were escaping from the poison bombs. These people climbed to the highest floors of buildings because the gas would settle on the lower floors, and so they died in the bombing instead. And I wanted to ask him why all this was happening but my tongue wouldn't move, and my eyes were blurry, and I thought of what my brother had said to my mother once, on one of the first days when he came home with torn clothes, and she yelled at him not to go out and protest anymore, and told him the Mukhabarat would kill him at once if they picked him up. My mother was crying ... my brother went out to the protests. This was a long time ago, maybe two years or more, and planes back then weren't bombing houses or dropping poison gas. I don't understand how a giant plane can come and kill small, weak people in such quantities.

A story, when I want to write it and draw it, seems understandable when it's about a large beast that eats people. But a plane! Is this what planes do?

My hair was wound around my neck, and Hassan was spraying me with water. He went away and moved around the bodies and I saw his shadow, then he came back to me and whispered *You're safe, dear.* I could see tears gushing from his eyes as he left me and started spraying water on the other bodies.

I am trying to define the sounds that I could hear, but I can't! Because there was shouting and screaming and coughing, and strange words. There were gasping sounds, and lots of phantoms penetrated my hearing and they were no help in working out what was going on. There was a room soaked in water and we were swimming in it like paintings, and there were souls rising to heaven, children and women and men, more children and women than men. I was able to tell the souls apart from each other. At that moment, I thought about the picture I had always imagined of what it would be like when our souls rose to heaven. The souls were lined up like this, but there was no other resemblance between the picture I had thought I would be in and this watery image that got bigger and bigger as I woke. I fainted and came back and I opened my eyes and was dizzy again.

The last time, before Hassan took me and carried me away, he went out quickly and I heard a strange noise and a din, and I was trying to feel my fingers, since I felt like I didn't have a body except for my eyes and my ears. I brought my middle fingers up to my eyes, and they weren't clear but I could see them, and then I put them in my mouth and bit them. My mother used to say that if you are in a dream and you think you are dreaming, bite your fingers, and it used to make me laugh. I put my fingers in my mouth and bit them with my teeth. It was real and I felt the pain from the bite, but it was a faint pain even though I kept pressing down on the fingers with my teeth. I had confirmed that I wasn't just eyes and ears, like the Cheshire Cat in Wonderland when he disappears and his eyes reappear. I was whole! And I planned to raise my head again to see the rest of the bodies lying on the floor but I couldn't separate my head from the water-soaked floor, I could only splash it around in the water.

Everyone was spraying water, they were doing it constantly. The shouting and the din around me was continuous, and when I turned my face and opened my eyes, I saw the woman. Her face was looking at me and her eyes were open, and an orange-coloured stream was coming out of her mouth, and one of them yelled *That woman's dead, get her up from there.* And the phrase *There is no god but God* was repeating on lots of muttering lips. They never stopped repeating it, over and over, all the time.

No one turned to the man who asked for the woman to be moved. He was carrying a piece of paper in his hand, and writing. Despite his blurry outlines, he seemed like an alien in this room where souls rose to heaven. I will leave him out of the impressionist painting I have decided I will make of this odd place, one day in the future. He was wearing things made out of plastic and he put a camera on his back. He came up to the woman's face and took a picture of it, and I was looking into her open eyes and her open mouth, where I could even see her teeth. She was close to me and there were voices rising all around me, there were bodies of women thrown all around me, and the women were dead, and they were wearing all their clothes but they were soaked with water.

I turned my face to the other side and there was another woman's face. A blue face. She seemed to be sleeping, and I wanted to scream *I am here and I'm not dead!* I tried to shout but my tongue stayed in place. I wanted to move my fingers but there were fingers on top of mine. Cold fingers. I didn't dare move, perhaps I was dead and I didn't know it. Hassan had disappeared, and the bodies of the women piled up all around me. I closed my eyes then fingers came up to my face, and a person stood up, someone unfamiliar ... covering my hair, he carried my head in his hands and I held my breath. Do you know what fear is? Fear is not being able to breathe, that's all it is! He put a hijab on me, and shifted me a little bit, then he moved the woman next to me, and her fingers ended up on my stomach, and I stopped breathing. I thought that this was dying, and that all I had to do now was stop myself breathing and I would enter death. How much time passed? I don't know. But I started breathing again slowly, and I didn't open my eyes. I hid from the eyes of the women around me. An intense cold seeped into my body then took hold of me by the fingertips, as if I was turning into a statue of ice. This happens in stories. The Snow Queen turns people into ice, and now I was turning into ice. The ice reached halfway up my body, and I closed my eyes again. I died several times. Every minute, I died a different way then came back to life. I lost the ability to open my eyes. I felt limp and lethargic. Now, when I think of those seconds where I believed that this was death, I think of lethargy coming gradually, a deep and delicious feeling in the head, coming from somewhere remote, rising slowly, then plunging me into an empty abyss. The abyss was bottomless but it was wonderful, as if I was falling softly from a mountain peak, as if gravity had transformed into something like the palm of a hand. I have read about the moments before dying. I mean, in the novels I used to devour (and I do love the word *devour*, I prefer it to saying *I read*). As you know (or perhaps I forgot to tell you), my mother used to say I was a bookmouse who nibbled pages into tiny pieces. I used to imagine myself as a mouse; I am very familiar with them. They lived in the courtyard of the house where we lived, and we killed lots of them, and once my mother took out a small mountain, or rather a pile, but anyway, back then my mother took out a small pile of shredded paper from under my bed and cursed the hour that God had afflicted her with such a mad daughter. I used to stuff the pages I drew on into the gaps between the piles of things my mother crammed under the bed to give us more space inside the room. The pile of papers that the mouse had nibbled through was a twenty-page story I had written and drawn and coloured in, and I spent the rest of the day crying and I wouldn't move from the bed. Actually, I wasn't crying only for my pages that the mouse had nibbled up, but because I had forgotten how to go back and write that story again.

What I wanted to tell you was about death. And about the paradox that I am still trying to understand of those moments when I was limp with the horrible smells still in my nose, and I was swimming in the water with a group of dead women, and they were gathered all around me and they smelled odd as well. But that moment of limpness after one of the men stood up to cover my face and hair because they thought I was dead, and fingers ended up on my stomach (the fingers of the dead woman I told you about), that moment, the one that I'm trying to explain now while recalling everything I have ever read about dying in books, was nothing like any moment I had read about, and I hadn't imagined that I would be able to feel it because I know there are gaps in my mind, gaps put there *by the will of God the Mysterious*, as my mother used to say. I had a plan a long time ago, it was this: to write and illustrate a long novel (it's a shame to write it with no colours or pictures). I think the right moment for turning these words into drawings is coming. Inside every event is motion, so I say to myself. It's not necessary for an event to be inside a square frame. I used to think we could arrange the colours in illustrations so they would become part of one larger canvas that continued over every page, and the black, sharp-cornered lines of the words would disappear and colours would settle in their place. I don't know why I am going back over these things now, when I am writing about waiting for Hassan and explaining to you about the moments when I died for the fourth time and then lived again. Perhaps it was the water. Yes, the water was the real reason that pushed me to it, the water that the corpses were floating in. They weren't really floating, but I felt like they were. They were still spraying water on most of the bodies, and I was dying and falling into a delicious limpness. I wasn't thinking of anything, that was what I wanted to say to you. I knew that I was dying. Everyone around me was dying. I saw several children go limp and close their eyes, and there was a man shouting at his son while spraying him with water: *Baba, don't go to sleep.* And I saw the boy close his eyes and sleep. I saw them all do this. They were trying to wake a group of lumps, limp and swinging in the water. The strange lumps seemed like watercolours, they were the bodies of men and women and children, and other lumps a short distance away were people who were shouting and shaking their heads or their hands or their arms. These last ones I didn't look at, but I could hear their voices. During those moments, I couldn't look at anything. There was only the ceiling. For moments, perhaps minutes, I was falling into a wonderful sleep, which didn't mean anything other than the quiet I dreamed of. I knew I was dying and I wasn't angry or afraid, I was pleased, and the ceiling above me was the sky, and there was a white fan hanging from the ceiling, not moving (perhaps the electricity was cut off), and on the ceiling was tattered paint. I could see all this despite the twilight in my eyes, but it was turning to clouds, and I wasn't thinking of anything, and everything I had read about the moments before dying and moving to the other world hadn't been true because I felt a pleasant surrender and I wasn't thinking of what was happening around me, or even the reason for my being there. Even the question that used to make me spin round on myself was missing, and that question was: Has the world always been this way? Is this what it's really like? I didn't know, because I have always been tied in my room. Does that other world in the middle of Damascus really exist—our lane and our house? Is that world still standing? Has it disappeared and turned into a world of stories and pictures? How do people live there and go on like normal while what is happening here is happening? I wonder this now, but back then I was only tumbling into the darkness. The shadow was gluey and the water didn't intervene at all. The black corridor my eyelids closed onto was also narrow and gluey, blended with blue dots ... pustules that I felt were eating my eyes. I am trying to remember the story as it happened. And so I went with the darkness and the shadow into my death.

I woke up and Hassan was slapping me on my face and shouting like the men had shouted before, and this is what made me certain that I was dying. *Wake up, wake up ...*

Don't go to sleep ... I felt his hands around my hand, his fingers! Imagine, I felt his fingers, and they were swooping down onto my face, and then his fingers took hold of mine and rubbed them. The men around him scolded him and demanded that he get back and respect the hurma of the women. A faraway voice said *These are women, get away from there! Cover your eyes!* And Hassan was shouting at them: *They're dead!* Then he slapped me again. Now, after time has passed, I realise I was angry that he had woken me up and he hadn't let me fall peacefully into the gluey shadow. The glueyness was calm and sweet, you walk into it as if you are nothing. Nothing. It was my fourth attempt at dying. I have discovered recently that life is just practise for what it feels like to die. Everything that happens is just practice, like you might practise drawing or painting.

I thought, just now, of drawing a picture of death. Before, I used to believe that drawing was more capable of expression than words, and that lines and curves and corners and colours were more responsive to me than words, but I still couldn't imagine what a drawing of death would look like. Now, after the appearance of death, I know that it is a white page turning black, watercolours deepening through different shades of black, then turning white again within a few seconds. Death is those black seconds that contain a small red dot inside them. The red dot is the gateway to death. I could feel these black seconds before I opened my eyes, and the red dot was right in front of me, and I felt my eyelashes sticking to it, but a faint light began to seep in from a distance, a light that was blended with black threads, with giant black ropes (but they were only my eyelashes that were tangled together), then I broke through the black ropes and found the light. My body was no longer there, it had evaporated. There were soft spots running in the area of light in front of my eyes. Sounds came back, but I didn't move. If I'd moved, something would have come out of my insides. Hassan took hold of my fingers and I breathed, and the shadow saturated with horrible smells came out. It came out of my stomach and my eyes. I was looking into

Hassan's eyes. They were clear. To be more precise, they were moist with water. You know what it means when eyes are moist with water, they call it *tears*.

How I love words and their meanings!

I was swimming in the water and it reached halfway up my backside, and fingers were piling up around me, fingers soaked with water from the women's bodies.

When I opened my eyes and saw the ceiling that seemed for an instant to be raining flakes of paint, and water was pouring again, that was the moment I came back to life. That moment, which I can tell you about, was happiness. I used to have a book that Sitt Souad found under President's Bridge in the middle of Damascus. My brother called the place Revolution Bridge later on, as I told you before, but when Sitt Souad brought the book, the bridge was still President's Bridge. The book was strange. It was called *Fiqh Al-Lugha* and it was a kind of dictionary written by a man called Al-Tha'alibi, a scholar who lived about a thousand years ago. I loved his name, which was like *tha'lib*, the word for "fox," and I imagined him walking with a red fox by his side, like the fox in *The Little Prince*. I discovered happiness when I started this book, right from the first page—this was two and a half years ago, at the beginning of winter. I could turn the strange and difficult meanings found in that book into pictures, but here in the cellar there are no colours. I have grey, black, and white … no … there's no white here. There is only one colour here, and that is the colour of dust, but I understand colours through words, so I am going back to my favourite book, which is still on top of my box in our house. I drew Al-Tha'alibi's face and, what a surprise! it was red. And next to it I drew a red fox. Once, I drew him with the Little Prince and next to them I drew the fox that they both shared, and I drew a little story in between them. I wished it really was part of the story of *The Little Prince*. The story is still at home, and it is a discussion between the Little Prince and Al-Tha'alibi about the sky. I don't know if you have read the first sentence in this book, the one that explains meanings, but I am afraid of the meanings of things when they turn into words, as it is hard for me to understand bare words without turning them into pictures. So when I read the first line in Al-Tha'alibi's book—*Everything that is above you and provides you with shade is the sky*—it changed my life! It was the first time I had read such a dictionary. I read encyclopedias of art and science, and normal dictionaries, but it was the first time that I had been immersed in an explanation of the meanings of words, and it was amazing.

How can people feel miserable when they possess such a gigantic quantity of meanings?

Do you know, since that moment the whole world has become my property? The roof of my house became sky, and the roof of this cellar is sky also, and the covers, when I bury myself underneath them and draw, are sky. Everything that is above me is sky. And in this way you can create an entire world of words. In the past, whenever I was trying out a game with words, I never stopped drawing, then I started to love drawing pictures with words.

All of this talking just so I can tell you about the happiness that came suddenly when I was looking at the shabby hospital ceiling that rained flakes of paint on us. I wasn't looking at the ceiling, I was seeing the sky. Everything that was over me, that shaded me, was sky. I was imagining its burning sun, and my gaze travelled far away ...

Hassan picked me up and took me out of the watery room, then he ran with me and put me in front of the steps to the hospital and I leant my head on the wall. I was in a half-sitting position and he started to wipe my face, and I was looking at the actual sky. The door was open, and this happiness that arrived in bursts made me wish that the world would continue as it was, because Hassan was gently coming close to me, and trying not to handle me roughly, and I wasn't seeing the visions that came and went, and there was no shouting or screaming, and the roar of that plane I had seen far away in the sky had disappeared, and I was looking and I saw only skies above me. Hassan's face and his eyes and the blue sky were all skies, and all the electricity poles I could see had turned into skies too, and I wasn't sad. My fingers began to twitch and my vision started to clear. There and then, I saw everything around me. Through the open door, I could see a doctor wearing all white and three women around him wearing the same colour. They were moving like four white lines, leaping between the bodies, and a man was holding a water hose and sprinkling a group of bodies. The water had no colour and the hose was red. Then another doctor came in, all in white, and he was crying as he carried some glass tubes in his hand and wrote something on them, then he asked a young man who was standing nearby if he could lift the body he had been sitting next to; they were gathering the bodies in a corner away from the corridor, and the doctor carried on writing and crying. The distant corner was growing and the doctor was moving about and talking quietly and giving instructions to the young men, including Hassan. Hassan carried bodies and put them in the corner, then he stood next to the doctor, and people were running and jumping. They went out and came back in, and bodies were flung at the entrance to the hospital and bodies came out of the hospital, and I couldn't make out anything anymore apart from the white colour of the doctors and nurses moving around, and a woman standing opposite me, three children lying at her feet. She was wearing grey, her hijab and all her clothes were all pale grey. She was standing in front of the bodies of the three children, staring at them. She was like a stone, she didn't blink and she didn't move. The people coming in and going out bumped into her, but she didn't move. She didn't quiver. Her eyes were on the bodies of the children, and there was a man coming up to me and holding her and trying to move her, but she wouldn't move. He screamed *Oh God!* and the women didn't turn and only kept on staring. Her face was yellow. She was close to me. I turned my head to the other side and when I tried to take another look at her, she had disappeared and the man was asking *Where did the mother go? Where did the mother of the children go?* No one was answering him. He was screaming and hugging the three children who were lying there as if they were sleeping, a weird calm on their faces. I was frightened. They were wearing pyjamas that all looked the same but each one was a different colour—red and orange and yellow—three colours lying in the water ... I heard voices coming from the microphones in the mosques, they were asking for covers and blankets, and the voices didn't stop, and I closed my eyes and would have liked Hassan to lay me down in the water again but I saw him taking pictures of the bodies, jumping between them, then the colours started to mix and I couldn't tell them apart and I shut my eyes. It wasn't the limpness, I was just sleeping. There weren't any colours in my sleep.

DO YOU KNOW, I woke up one day and saw that I was a light hanging from the ceiling, and I was swinging inside a piece of white cardboard, pure white, and this light was like the light that Sitt Souad used to hang in the middle of her room? I remember it was the first time in my life I had seen anything like it. It was a small light dangling from a delicate string, and around the light was a white lampshade. The white shade was placed over the light and I was amazed it was so large and that it was decorated in such a painstaking manner. Then afterwards, I saw a lot of it, in photography books as well, and when I woke up I was in the cellar and I saw this same lampshade. The details of the holes in the lace were the same, but Sitt Souad's lampshade was large (or so I thought), and I was a small lampshade. Light was coming from a distance, and I was trying to open my eyes and imagine what was happening and why I was here but the light was sharp and it stopped me from seeing anything, and the lampshade restricted my movements. I lifted my head to see what was happening outside the lampshade, and Hassan came back into view. He was sitting next to me, looking at me but not looking at me at the same time. I was lying on a bed, and my head and my body had a cover on them that was red and smelled dirty. Hassan was moving his lips and talking to me, but I couldn't hear anything so I turned my eyes away again and saw, from the edge of the cellar window, a piece of sky. It was blue and clear, as usual. Then I noticed there were women and children in the opposite corner, sleeping. Two women were cleaning the cellar and Hassan was helping them. Three children were lying down, and my hand was tied to the bars of the high window. You have to imagine now, as you are reading the words of this new story that has entered the original story (I supposed that something would happen, because there were people all around me), that this cellar is a large blank piece of paper and we are its ridiculous lines—parallel, curving, intersecting lines created by our eyes and noses. Similarly, you must imagine that I was a small, straight line, parallel to the straight line that was the sponge mattress. I would have preferred this bed to be flipped so it was like a wall, and I would be sitting on it, like the wall of the Little Prince in the story. Then you must imagine that the sleeping children were like circles rolled up around each other. Everything else formed a space that was made incomprehensible by the overlapping of the colours, because the lines intersected and came together, and points crossed them that were impossible for me to understand. And in front of the bed there were stacks of cartons which, it later became clear, were large pieces of cardboard used by the printer whose cellar we were in. I hoped that when I was able to touch them, they would all be transformed into colourful stories. But as I told you, the only colour available here is blue.

The two women started wiping and cleaning our faces and they carried on moving something around that was boiling on the small gas ring. I let them do whatever they wanted to take care of me, and when I opened my eyes for the second time I discovered the place was much cleaner. There was a fabric cover in the middle of the room, and on it were some newspapers, and in the middle of those were some vegetables, two rolls of bread, and a cup of apple juice. I was hungry but I needed to pee. I tried to explain this to the two women, then I realised that I had already done it in my clothes, more than once. I smelled horrible, and the women were looking at me doubtfully even though they didn't look any better than me. They didn't speak to me. They were red-eyed and stared into space, and moved like worn-out dolls. I couldn't understand why they were here, although the bombing hadn't stopped and Hassan had disappeared from sight. I closed my eyes during one of their fits of passion for cleaning me and moving me around like another doll. They were trying to open my lips and pour some drops of water down my throat. I clamped my teeth shut and turned into a piece of wood. I was frightened; I believed I could speak. Perhaps you guessed from the beginning of my story that I was frightened, but I am worried that you are one of those who reads and expects clear, direct, ready-made words, and who doesn't like the games of stories. So I say to you that I was aware I had been wetting myself in my clothes since the moment Hassan dragged me over the dirt, shouting *Chemical!* That was an expression I didn't understand at the time, because to me *chemical* just meant a chemical substance that girls would study at school from Grade 7 (or maybe Grade 8, I can't remember now), and I didn't understand the enormity then of what was happening.

THAT DAY, I discovered I was just a lump of disgusting smells. I smelled the stink, and saw the strange looks the two women gave me as they stared at the rope reaching from the window bars to my wrist and my body, and felt their resistance to looking after me. Then I closed my eyes again before getting up and pointing outside. I put my hand on my hip and motioned to them that I wanted to pee. They stood up in alarm and brought some clothes.

There was a big black bag placed next to the children and it contained some clothes. That meant there were six of us and we had a black bag, and things here made it a little home. The two women began to wipe my body with a rag soaked in water, and they were crying all the time, and they changed my clothes, then one of them went outside and threw them into the street. I was looking at the street because my head reached the level of the window if I climbed on top of the packs of paper, and I could see a bit of the outside. The woman threw the clothes and hurried back down the cellar steps—she was panting. Cats circled round the clothes and I closed my eyes again, and soon I was wearing different clothes, then one of the women took my hand and led me to a nook where there was a toilet, and closed the door. The rope was long enough for me to reach the third step of the cellar stairs, and for me to pee. Pooing was a big problem. The water had been cut off since the beginning of the siege and that wasn't good—but I didn't poo, I just peed. It smelled awful. My stomach was empty, but strangely I wasn't hungry when I woke up the second time, even though we had been here for days, from what I heard the women saying. I have already forgotten their faces. I was throwing up strange liquids. My throat was burning and my eyes hurt and I felt dizzy, and everyone in the cellar was suffering from the same symptoms. The children spent most of the time asleep. I couldn't work out how old they were; they were like lumps curled around themselves. I told you a little while ago that the shapes of the children made circles among the collection of lines formed by the sketches of the cellar, but I wasn't able to include them in this story, I mean in this part of the story of the cellar, or the other stories. I like saying *the other stories*—it means that beings are staying here with me, others are surrounding me, and that means I will be safe. Before all of this I wasn't worried, and I don't know what changed because Hassan came back twice and stayed for a few minutes. He brought some stuff and said he would come back to take us somewhere else. The third time he came back I woke up because he was shouting, and I was on my own in the room, and he was trying to wake me up. I don't find it easy to describe Hassan to you, because he is a story by himself, and it's a story that needs deep concentration. His story, where he came from, I don't known. Pictures of him creep into my head, pictures of his hair, and his rifle, his clothes, his eyes, his arms, the camera hanging at his middle. Every part of Hassan is a story, and his shirt was blue, which is odd. Because this blue colour was radiant despite the dust, it was like the colour of the pen I am writing with. I could feel him blazing, and it wasn't the blue of his shirt, but his eyes. This glow of his alternated between flaming up and swinging back and forth, and it turned my heart into scattered circles. Have you understood how I can explain things? Simply, I say *my heart*. I don't understand why the meanings of things blend into each other when the story of Hassan comes up. I think I am always thinking about him and he moves under my skin like blood, he and all his colours. He was constantly angry and his anger would live in my mind. He controlled it from the moment he picked me up and ran through the dust whirlwinds and we went past the violet houses (I say *violet* to you and you have to trust it, because the house walls had turned funny colours from the gas bombs) and I felt happy. Even though I am taking you back to a story of a dangling head and violet houses, I must confess through this chain of stories that this was one of the happiest moments I have ever known. There was something leaping in my chest on the left side.

Things don't exist before you feel them. I didn't understand what it meant to discover that something in your chest moves like a rabbit! I have read lots about this sensation, and when I learned it I was afraid. I had imagined this feeling in my head while I was reading about it, but actually knowing it was a different matter. These things between writing and drawing and truth ... they confuse me, they make me afraid.

I am really afraid. I am waiting here and these thoughts that don't turn into drawings will only come out in the form of words.

It's not true that it's in the shape of a rabbit, exactly. I mean, what jumps in my chest.

I would draw a fish if it was up to me, a fish jumping from a pond then falling onto the bank and panting because it misses the water! That is how the sensation was jumping about inside me. It had the outlines of a fish, its shape and its panting. I don't know whether I'm allowed to say that a fish pants. Because panting isn't something that fish do, but I suppose you know what I mean.

I am writing about Hassan for you, and I am observing the flies around me, coming out of the fish in my head. The sensation is settling in my ribs on the left side. Imagine me watching the flies all around me, and thinking there is a fish jumping between my ribs, and suddenly a fish shape wearing a rabbit skin leaps out from my chest and comes to rest! Drawing is better than words. If I had my paints, I could make you understand me much more clearly. Really, I would have preferred silence to drawing, and to look straight at you so you would know what I want, but that is impossible. We have to choose the least worst option, and here and now, waiting for Hassan, I choose the least worst option once again and I go on writing the meanings of the things around me because

I have lost part of the long chain of thought that is coiling up on my clay planet.

I didn't work out how long we stayed with the families in the cellar. I think I said to you before how many of them there were. I would wake up and go back to sleep, and they were arranging things around me. There was also hot lentil soup. We ate it for days at a time. Hot lentil soup and bread.

I am trying to understand while I am writing to you. I imagine you with two long horns and eyes of fire and you are reading these words of mine, then I think that maybe you are nothing ... same as I was before the world turned upside down on my head when I escaped my mother's hand. Perhaps the world was already like this before I ran away from my mother. But I know the world, and it is a secret that no one else knows. My secret is that I have known the world all along. I really did know the outside world, because of my muteness, and you're probably surprised by that but I assure you that I learned all about the world by stopping my tongue from moving. And through books. And that was enough for me, and I was happy. I think my life began back to front, because Paradise was there, where silence was ... Then suddenly, what happened, happened.

Before I woke up, I would open my eyes to watch what they were doing, the people Hassan left me with. Who were they? Lots of strangers have passed through my life recently. The two women disappeared and I saw a new group of people. They were homeless like me, and we didn't learn much about each other. There was a woman crying and she would put her child on her legs and wrap some clothes into a cushion shape. Then she sang a soft lullaby to the baby. The sound of a hamza was continually coming out from her lips: 'a-'a-'a-'a-'a ... 'a-'a-'a-'a-'a ... She would look at the cellar window. The bombing went on constantly and the child was looking towards the window, like her. She held his hand and bent over him quietly, and the child was completely resigned. He didn't move, he didn't cry. I would be woken up by the thunder of the bombs and I could feel my body trembling while he closed his eyes peacefully and his mother held the tips of his fingers. They stayed in the corner away from everyone else, and the mother would lean her back against the huge pile of cardboard packages.

During those strange awakenings, I would think of my mother's legs. The woman would spread out her legs and make them into a cradle. She put the child's head by her feet and rocked him gently and murmured some songs. For an instant I would think that I was the thing lying over the legs that had turned into a huge bed for me, and that it was my mother singing those songs. I remember she used to do the same thing until I was four, looking gravely at the window and shaking her legs rhythmically, but I remember it like something that doesn't belong to me, in a place I don't know.

The mother who used to look at the cellar window was staring at the remaining piece of sky. In my mind, there was no sky outside. That small piece was the sky that I had raised myself. It even proved the opposite—that the earth had no sky other than the part seen from the window. Even the colours that surrounded us as we were crammed into the cellar had no importance, as I didn't see any of them apart from the colours that have no colour.

I would sneak glances at Hassan's movements among us while he was bringing things and taking things away, then while he was cleaning his weapon. The colours were like your eyes between a quick blink and a sudden stare at a black spot. Perhaps you could say that the colours were all grey, and all the colour of cement. You could only make out the colour black. The two women were dressed in it, and I heard the other woman say she wanted to go outside, and she looked at me with pity and hostility. It seemed that I was the problem. Hassan quietly asked them to be quiet. The bombs weren't stopping and he had to go out. He would come for a short time and quickly go away again.

THE LAST TIME I opened my eyes I desperately wished I could retreat back inside their lids. I jumped up, terrified. I love these clear feelings—I was really, actually terrified. The cellar was empty and dark but there was enough dim light creeping from the sky to see the shadows. I knew I was alone. I didn't notice the shaking of the mother's feet, and I couldn't hear her singing. Again, they had left me in the cellar.

I can't fully describe my feelings at that moment. You don't know what the cellar was like. I was alone there. I think I wet myself in my clothes again, and I was hungry.

There was something difficult to explain and make clear to you, and that is that I had never been forced to feel need for anything before. This was a secret joy, because I was feeling hungry, and it was a feeling that belonged to me alone. I don't remember ever eating because of hunger before. If I had colours and rulers and pages, I would make you see that the situation is like a straight line with no colours, and it isn't white. Although I would have preferred to draw it using a white line on black paper.

I could feel an itch between my thighs. There were things crawling over my legs, and I didn't dare move because the silence was soured by the thunder of distant bombs. I sat up and leant my back on the wall, and my vision began to widen. The place was as it had always been. Only the people had disappeared. If only they had untied me before they went! This was something that made me certain Hassan would come back.

I jumped onto the window ledge and stood on tiptoe so I could see the street. But it wasn't enough.

I had to drag a cardboard box in front of the window and step on it—it was full of paper, and I hoped it was tall enough to raise me so I could see the street. But that wasn't enough either. The packs of paper that were high enough for me to see the street had been put too far away.

I opened the window. It must have been dawn because the sky was turning violet, my favourite colour. It made me feel happy. I don't have to remind you every time that it was the colour I saw when my head was dangling from Hassan's shoulders, and it is the colour that they say is the result of the poison gas that the planes drop (or so people kept saying when they were running away that night). I must admit I was surprised by this, because the colour was very beautiful and I don't understand how a colour can kill people. In those moments, when I was watching the colour of the sky that was like the colour of death, I started crying. I didn't understand what was happening to me. My needs were clear: I was frightened and I was crying and I was hungry, and what was happening now wasn't at all possible for me to understand. I had never realised that I could feel these things before. I knew why I was crying, I understood it, and I felt I needed to move my tongue, but I also didn't understand why my tongue was going round in my throat, and I started to hear a strange stammering sound, not a scream, when a cat came along the street. I wasn't afraid of it. I found its eyes right in front of mine and there was a movement … a strange movement in front of me. I didn't see it clearly, but the cat jumped in front of me and ran away and the violet colour in the sky was turning blue. The street was completely empty. I could crane my head. I brought over a second box full of paper and I was a little higher and my head was now free in the air. The street was long and narrow, and the houses were completely destroyed. The morning smell was odd, the street was filled with rubbish and rubble from the buildings … There was no colour here. Just a cement colour with white and grey dust. The thing that was moving now became clear, opposite the window where my head was freed. It was a skinny dog, almost yellow; its tail was brown. The light shone and the sky had no clouds. Perfect, pure blue. I describe colours carefully, I think my eyes exist through knowing and detailing colours. At that moment, the blue of the sky was perfect, without shading— clear, pure blue, cut up by the broken lines of the remnants of destroyed buildings. The street was abandoned. There was no trace of any living being, except for the cat, which had run away, and the dog, which was digging among the heaps.

As I write this, I am breathing so loudly I can hear it. My tongue is moving inside my mouth and I feel ready to talk to any living thing. I want to walk. Between the blue and the morning, I am thinking and my eyes are filled with water. I can taste the salt in my tears, and I am thinking about Hassan. Only he is in my mind, even my mother and brother's images have disappeared, and so has everything else around me. Everything has gone away. Maybe death has taken Hassan, like it did my mother and brother. And this is confusing for me, that people disappear suddenly like this, as if they had never been. I have thought about this matter a lot, and I also know that it's no good spending time thinking about it, because in the end we can't keep existing forever. This also means that I am not forced to carry on living. Will that ever change? It will save us only from feeling what is going on around us. How simple and easy that is.

So, as I was watching the dog, I leaned my face on the window bars. The glass was shattered. I was trying to stare at what the dog was doing. Its ribs showed beneath its skin; it was a very skinny dog. It was digging around in the rubble across the street from me, which used to be a four-storey building and had now turned into a mountain of cement. Probably several bombs had hit it. There are times when spots float up to my skin, then swim back underneath. I can feel them when my eyes are closed, and when I want to make sure they are there I touch my fingers against my skin and feel them, but I can't see them. That moment, when I was touching my skin, I turned my cheek in the direction of the four paws of the dog while it dug among the piles, throwing up puffs of dust behind it. I couldn't see it directly, and because I believed that people had been more or less correct in calling me strange, I tried not to avert my eyes from the head of the dog, which seemed closer than it should be. A leap or two and it would be right in front of my face, so I retreated and brought my head back underneath the cellar's ceiling. Then the sharp roar of the plane began. The dog stopped. It raised its head. It turned round and round and I ducked a little; perhaps it knew I was there, it had that humble look but there was no spark in its eye, I saw that clearly. The sun lit the place up, and its rib bones and its skinniness showed even more clearly. It moved inside a pile of cement, and the dust appeared, and I heard a strange sound moving from the opposite side; it was the meow of a cat. Terrified, the cat escaped right in front of me, running away quickly. The dog stood and watched it listlessly, then carried on digging. You can imagine the scene: a girl like me, reaching her head out of a window. I have to describe the scene outside to you, and it's hard to do, but we can draw a building. I know that the building above us was destroyed totally. There are piles of rubble in front of me but they aren't large like the piles across the street, so I can still look left and right. This means there is a dog opposite me, and an enormous pile, and the dog is wagging its tail slowly and digging around in the dirt. And two cats scurry away and escape, then I hear the roar of the plane, but that can't be seen on the page. We can add the shape of the plane. I had never seen the planes that dropped bombs before. Once, I looked at the sky before we moved here, and they said *That's a plane.* Drawing it is easy. But imagine that the girl is inside now, which means that the moment I will describe to you is coming up. Don't assume anything about that girl's head, and don't forget that the girl is me. I have taken off my head covering and my head is free, which means that I won't be able to add any other touches to the girl's head, because her hair is hanging down. This is all taking place underneath the cellar ceiling but even if the hair was outside, I wouldn't draw it in a special way because there is no wind, and so I can't draw flying locks of hair. The heat had been stifling since the morning, and here, so it can appear more precisely, I must describe the dog to you, in addition to its skinniness, and its slow movements, and its dull, humble eyes. It was determined to get its jaw inside the rubble, and when it went further inside half its body disappeared, then it began to drag something out.

When I heard the roar of the plane again, then the thunder of the bomb, it wasn't far away but I couldn't see any trace of it. The dog looked at the sky. We were alone, me and the dog. There was a ray of sunshine falling entirely on him, and before he ran away and disappeared I saw the thing he had been digging for in the rubble. It is not drawn here. It was a small hand, a real hand. It was in the skinny dog's jaws. Its colour wasn't clear, like the colour of the cement—but the dog, as it escaped the roar of the plane and the thunder of the bombs, tilted to the side a little and slipped in the street. It was a lane really, because the distance from the cellar to the opposite building wasn't more than ten feet I think, maybe a little more or less, but that hand and the dog's jaw passed in front of my face for a second or so as it circled, and I could see the fingers because it was carrying the hand so that the fingers were sticking out while its jaw gripped the palm at the other end, staining the front of its jaw with blood and dust. I saw it. It was just a few seconds, as I said, but time stopped in that moment. I had dried my sweat some minutes before with my sleeve, and I heard the sound of my snot moving, and I was sniffing because there was a trail coming out of my nose. I hadn't thought that I could stare with such curiosity. I watched the dog while I reached my head through the window, then I tried to stare at the pile of earth in front of the building. There was no trace of anything there. As I was reaching my head out, the dog disappeared from sight, fingers still in its jaw, and the plane's roar was sharp and clear. Before I could feel anything, there was a heavy wind that threw me onto the ground and a weird noise that I couldn't identify or even look to see what was making it, because a cloud of dust was floating above me and I was falling to the ground. I felt a strange heat coming out of my eyes. I felt drowsy straight after the cloud of dust, and I fell asleep.

DO YOU KNOW what the secret planets are? Like a magic hat from stories that makes you disappear. No one can reach you ... You can try it! Let's suppose it's important to you, but all this must be learned by heart, because the magic recipes I am supplying to you might burn up ... or I might decide to rip them up. It all depends on Hassan coming back. Hassan, who isn't coming back.

Back then, I found it hard to open my eyes. I believed that I was on one of my secret planets, and that no human being had reached it for days. Perhaps it was even longer than that. Or less. I don't remember anymore when the last day I ate was. The water ran out today. The water is cut off. There is no water in the siege. The water taps I have seen are covered in dust from the bombs, and the only tap in here (that I have tried to blow inside of several times) has run dry. The only available water you could think about drinking is in the toilet, and even then there's not much. On my obligatory secret planet (I can call it that because it doesn't belong to me, I didn't build it myself, even though it is still like the magic hat that makes you disappear), on this planet—the cellar—water is a dream.

There are secret planets I have always lived on that are different to this cellar, the current secret planet. I remember appointing it a secret planet when I opened my eyes and Hassan was wiping my face and my hair with his fingers and removing all traces of dust from them, and there were, as I told you, several stones that had come through the cellar window whose iron frame wouldn't budge.

Right now, I am still tied; this is a good sign. I won't move from my place, and I will stay here with Hassan, and I won't lose him like I lost my mother and my brother when I untied my rope at the checkpoint. Hassan said he was going out for a few minutes and then coming back, after the last bomb fell beside the cellar. The minutes became days, and lots of bombs have fallen one after another since then, and the door is still closed. He said he would close it for a few minutes, he would look at where the bomb fell and then come back, but the bombs have carried on falling and he hasn't come back.

How much time has passed? Time is just a long path on a cloud. The forest and the path are both carried on a planet, and I don't know how the cloud moves. Does it run? Does it stay in place, or rise upwards like the fairy ball? Since I went out with my mother to visit Sitt Souad, time has stayed suspended like the shadow of a plane on the clouds, and I am swimming in a sky, hanging between the space in the lampshade and the little path in the forest, and all the beings are around me, the beings of my second secret planet, which I'll tell you about later.

Time, like the time that passed before I was born, was nothing, and now again it is nothing. I don't understand it. I don't know it, and I stay hanging in a fixed point like clock hands turning in the wrong direction.

The earth now is like a giant clock. When Hassan comes, it will turn into branches forking off from the minute hand, the second hand, then suddenly the dividing branches will disappear into the forest, and the giant clock will turn back into a cloud and a path and a lampshade.

Under the bed, where I built my first secret planet, there was a blue colour. In the gap under the bed, there was another small bed that was mine; I made it, it was blue. The pillow was white, absolute white, its whiteness seemed to glow when it was surrounded by blue and black, and time used to ride over my head on the back of a beast whose kind eyes were brimming. Large, tear-filled eyes. Time was also a small fairy with butterfly wings and a mouse tail, and it wore short red-and-green-striped trousers, and its eyes were a blazing blue. That was time on my first secret planet. I used to look at it and know that making time into a fairy didn't really work because the word *fairy* is feminine, and *time*, in the language here, is masculine. But that's not important, because colours are what define the meanings of life, not necessarily sticking to words. Time there was different to the time that I have seen here.

There are different times, they change from one secret planet to another. Everything around me seems like it can change and mutate, and everything obeys strange laws. I believed, before, that time was a fairy and it would keep me company whatever I did. Is time the same when it doesn't mean anything to run away from the seconds along the forest paths that hover over my head? The tree branches would start winding around me once again when, slowly and painfully, I opened my eyes.

I have explained all this to you in order to go back to that point. Before Hassan disappeared, when I opened my eyes, I was hardly breathing and Hassan was cleaning me. I shut my eyes again. I was afraid of making him go away from me, which he would have done if he realised I had woken up. I promise you I was awake enough to let him, unusually for me, carry on cleaning my face and hair and clothes. I wanted to see his eyes again but I stayed firm, letting him finish what he was doing. I wasn't thinking of anything else, except that happiness that landed on me suddenly whenever he was around. I thought about, and I keep in my memory, the touch of his fingers on my cheek, of those fingers which are what keep me clinging on to life. You know how much I admired those fingers. It seems to be a mistake to judge what things are like from their outer appearance. His fingers talked, like my fingers, and I wanted to laugh, because at last I could be free, even if it meant my mother and brother disappearing. Perhaps that seems like a heresy, but it was true.

I let him go on with what he was doing while I was thinking of this secret planet of mine that isn't like any of the planets I've lived on before. I will explain it to you now and I hope you won't be bored, because I would like you to know what happened, and in case I stay alive, I would like not to forget these moments I am writing down, because I can't draw them and they will be lost in my mind, just as I have lost many details from my old life.

I must admit that I am writing with joy, and this language is good to me, the language that you will make allowances for while you think of a lonely girl tossed in a cellar and tied up there while planes continue dropping bombs. You will be kind ... won't you?

I have lived on several secret planets before. I separated them like the Little Prince did on his journey between the planets. He had his planets and I have my secret planets. I learned all this from him. I remember his conversations with his flower and, if I'm being honest, they made me a bit angry.

So ... there was a secret planet under the bed, as I told you a little earlier. The bed was my house and the secret planet was the empty space between the box that my mother hid under the bed and what was left of the space by the wall. I would cram myself in there, where I put my drawings and my books and my notebooks, and the planet was big enough for me to lie down on my stomach and draw. The borders of that planet finished at the four bedposts, but underneath, the roots of the planet (and my roots that were tangled with it) reached to bottomless depths. I used to draw the roots connected to the centre of the earth through a point in my head. I would do this while remembering Alice and her ability to change her size, and I drew her again in all her different sizes while she was wandering through Wonderland, and she looked like Sitt Souad. There, I started to draw *Kalila and Dimna*, my favourite classic book, which they used to study in schools in the old days, and its brown cover is still in my box.

This planet was the first and no one knows about it. I would hide it while my mother and brother were around. I painted it many times, before my mother wiped away the colours with water and horrible cleaning chemicals. There, in that planet, I learned to write the letters of the alphabet with coloured symbols. I have more than a thousand pages written with coloured drawings—they are still there. I wrote everything I wanted to say with coloured symbols.

Emptiness defined my planet, although its exterior was marked by the bedposts and the box of my secrets, which I emptied after my mother demolished it and was forced to put some sheets in it. But I still had the side of the box and I painted it in fire colours, so my mother rubbed the colours off and shouted and yelled at me. It was one of the rare times she was angry. The second time, I painted it with patterns from a drawing I copied out of one of Sitt Souad's large leather books that was about the crowns of columns. The patterns were part of a column head in one of the palaces of Seville, you must know them. My mother let the drawing stay and didn't clean it off the box, and I stayed there for hours when I realised. She would say to me that it was real ... it was a real thing. My brother pinched my cheek cheerfully and brought me more paints when he saw the box, and I was so pleased by the twinkle in his eye when he looked at my drawings, and the wide laugh that was drawn on his face as he traced his fingers over the box and its patterns. His eyes got wider and wider ... After that, I used to redraw some of the patterns and throw them in the corners of the room where we lived, just to see my brother's eyes grow and grow and turn into two balloons!

I think the box is still there. It forms one of the boundaries of my first secret planet. The world was beautiful and colourful there, in the square gap that didn't go beyond the four bedposts. I used to carry this world between my fingers, and I didn't even need to raise my head! Because my head was higher than my body, it was flying. It would see everything go back to its place then, and my fingers would brush the sky then go back under the bed. I would draw by myself, and sometimes I only needed to turn into the cat in Wonderland, the smiling Cheshire Cat. So I would close my eyes and things would fly to me and stay beside me, in the gap of the first secret planet.

Do you know how I was thrown out of it?

My mother decided to get some new pillows but she couldn't throw away the old ones, it was one of her habits. She never threw old things away for fear she might need them. Our house was a jumble of things we didn't need. My mother crammed the old pillows into that last corner under the bed, and she didn't appreciate my attempts to throw them away. My mother insisted on keeping them, even if she had to throw me out of the house instead, and she didn't explain it to me, she just turned me out from under the bed.

One of the few times I stuffed myself in there in an attempt to recapture my first place, we were cleaning the house and my mother threw all our things outside, and she scrubbed the floor of the room with horrible cleaning products. But while I was playing with the foam and the soap bubbles under the bed, I found no clue that would lead me back to that planet. It had disappeared completely, even though the pillows weren't there.

I drew it afterwards, after I lost it. And I gave my first secret planet a title (this was a few years later), and in the drawing I called it *Coloured Gap* and I really liked the title and I laughed out loud. I liked that it might make you think the gap was coloured, and this name became a new definition I gave to the word *rainbow*. I tried to remember exactly when I gave it this new name and I failed, as usual, but I put the drawing and the story of Coloured Gap in with my special papers, which, as you know, are still hidden in the box in our house. I will call it our house to make the difference between the house and my secret planet clear, because really, as I told you before: our house ... was just a single room.

My planet Coloured Gap, this rainbow, remained one of my most important secrets until I moved to my second secret planet, inside the library of Sitt Souad. The school library consisted of a large room and some pots holding different types of plants which Sitt Souad used to decorate the window. Aside from that, the library consisted of books and bookshelves lined up around the walls in every direction. In the middle of the room there was a large picture of the President, and next to it there was an equally large picture of his father. There were copies of these two pictures distributed everywhere in the school, including the corridors, and they were on large advertising boards in the squares in Damascus, and on the walls of houses. Everywhere I went, there were pictures of the President and his father. My brother used to say that statues of the father were distributed throughout every region of the country, but I have never seen them.

In the library, the two pictures covered what was left of the walls between the top bookshelf and the ceiling. In the headmistress's office (which I went inside once—I was with my mother when she went to object to a reproach from the headmistress for bringing me to school) I saw the same two pictures.

They were occupying the whole wall, two huge pictures of the President and his father. My mother said that the father of the President used to be our president, and the two pictures were framed in gold, clean and shining, and the men seemed huge, bigger than how they appeared on television.

Before I was stopped from going to the school, several bookshelves were added on top to make room for more books, everywhere except on the wall with the pictures. That room wasn't just mine, it was for all the students. Though it was mine sometimes. I would carry it in my head and it became part of another secret planet. Aside from the times, when I was five, when Sitt Souad would sit in there with me and teach me to read and write, I stayed there by myself. She would lock the door whenever she was forced to go out. And so, during classroom hours, I was ... a queen ... and that feeling used to strike me—the one that would make your chest swell and make you breathe in the air like you would die any minute ... before taking a huge gasp ... and letting out a laugh ... a loud laugh ...

On that secret planet that turned into a vast stage I forgot my tied hand. The stage was a semicircle inside the library. Beings would come out from the bookcases and turn the shelves into the boards of a stage. (I don't know stages very well but I have seen them on television and read about them in books.) The beings would scatter around me on every side and make a circle. They would slip out from the walls surrounding me; they would climb nimbly down the bookshelves. I don't know exactly when they appeared but I can tell you they would gather in a circle in crooked, circular rows whenever Sitt Souad closed the library door, and they would vanish as soon as she reappeared. Then the rows started to grow and get bigger until the place was stuffed with them and they started to sit on the shelves, and the ones that were left over would fly in the air. They turned themselves into shelves on top of the library shelves, and they kept methodically to their established places. They would form their rows around me—a small circle, and a bigger circle around that one. Every circle inside a circle. They piled on top of each other like spiral rows, but in an orderly way. They came out of the pages, waiting for their whole number to join them, and when they finished their conversation with me, they went back to their books. I must admit that they were very well mannered and never interrupted each other. Each one of them directed his speech to me, the rest were listening. Like this … and like this …

There was a secret agreement between us. They were like me. They didn't move their tongues, they didn't need to.

I am trying to remember the details of the library, my second secret planet. I doubt I can concentrate more than I already am. It used to be crowded with two white flying snakes, and with orange-coloured stars that moved between the rows, and characters that would vanish from time to time. And I saw paths in forests coming out from between the rows, and the whinny of horses going along them, and a loud din, and I was walking on the long forest path, squeezed between the characters who were arranged on either side of it, and strange beings would appear around me, and I would hear their voices in my head: two snakes with ostrich legs, a monkey with a giraffe head, and a rabbit with ostrich feathers. As for the camel, it had two small wings (like the wings of bats) at its neck. The paths would carry me; I wasn't walking, I would be standing still. Some plants dangling from the tree branches would take hold of me and they took me around the whole world. In the library, I would swim between the sky and the depths of the ocean. The colour of the sea wasn't blue. I have never seen the sea in my life, and I don't know whether it is blue down in its depths. It seems blue on the television, and in stories as well. But on that secret planet of mine, I saw it was translucent. I could feel the water surrounding me. I was breathing without bubbles. There were many paths and they would change from one day to the next. I was carried along these paths on Al-Bamatan, the blessed horse that carried Adam to Heaven, and I hung from the feather of a peacock, and I crossed hills and mountains with a single leap, and I could hold them inside my closed hands, and I smelled a disgusting smell sometimes, and I didn't like it at all. And there was the desert, after all this ... brown-skinned men and camel trains, and palm trees ... Pictures of oases overwhelmed me and sometimes they came out at me like cartoons ... the oases of Sinbad ...

On my second secret planet we became friends, me and the Little Prince. I learned from him how to build my planets just as he did. *I have to build planets*, he said to me while trying to get away from the crowding of the rows of beings. And I thought: *Planets!* I had already been living on my planets, he just gave me the directions. And we stayed friends. Perhaps more than friends.

This planet didn't disappear. It moved into my head, and there I learned to read books. Sitt Souad would sit me at the table and bring me one of the chairs crammed into the nooks between the shelves, then she would put her hand on my back and move it until my back was straight. She always used to say that I had to be absolutely ready in order to do reading and she refused to let me hunch my back as I turned the pages. She would bend over me and kneel down next to me while she spelled out the letters with me, then she made me pick up a pen and point to the words I was reading. Then she took my hand and said *Write*. I wouldn't pick up the pen at first, but when the second time she brought coloured pens, I picked them up and started to write the sentences in the shape of uneven words, and I did it again, then she made me memorise the story. It was amazing, because the process of reading and the process of writing would turn into disjointed tunes that came out like a whistle ... It was all just lips moving ... and I used to draw the letters and words in an exaggerated way while she laughed and watched me, repeating her usual phrase: *You're a genius, you have the soul of an artist!*

Along with the library planet and the planet under the bed, there is another secret planet in my head. This planet I have drawn a few times, and it is circle shaped. I have named it the Planet of Clay and I put some pages in it that others can't understand, and which I can't draw on in front of them. That planet stays closed and there are papers on it that no one has ever seen or touched, that's for sure! This planet is hard to invade. I would reach my hand to my head and open it up whenever I wanted to, and then it would be enough for me to close my eyes and the planet would grow and transform into a vast, limitless space. Back then, the world came to my planet and it wasn't me who wandered round it like I did in my previous planet in the library, which became the starting point for my head's journeys ...

Each one of my secret planets has its own importance, but the Planet of Clay has exceptional importance. This planet won't disappear until I disappear. This is good. My colour is like the colour of clay, in different shades. But at base I am clay coloured, and it is one of my favourite colours. We are toys made out of clay, small toys, quick to break and crumble, and in fact a simple scratch is enough to turn our bodies into dust. And our limbs are snapped so easily. You don't think so? You could have seen that for yourself when they bombed the house of Um

Saeed and the bomb fell next to her, and she turned into a half statue of clay. A statue with no legs. A toy with no legs. Um Saeed used to walk on two feet and she seemed like a mountain, and it was impossible to think of any miracle that was capable of wiping out such a mountain. Um Saeed turned into a legless clay toy in seconds, and her eyes were open in a strange way as if she was staring at somewhere in the distance, and her hands were spread wide, and her thobe was open to reveal her upper, naked half, which was quickly covered up before the men saw it. I didn't take a close look at where Um Saeed's upper half ended. I guess it was made up of coiling branches of red veins covered in clay, which crumbled afterwards. The rest of the bodies, the children and the mothers, I didn't see. The bodies had been scattered everywhere, and maybe they turned to dust. The bomb fell right on top of them. Their clay bodies disappeared. My mother used to say that bodies were eaten up by worms, and the torment of the grave that God had prepared for us was great, but I felt strange, because half of Um Saeed was turned to dust, and the other half would be eaten by worms. Do you see any difference there? The difference is that the worms will live a bit longer, then they themselves will turn into dust. If my mother heard me saying this, she would slap me. Even so, I know that my secret planet is in my brain. Inside its coils (which I haven't seen in real life, but I have seen a drawing of a brain in a science book in the school), it is just a clay room like a pit and inside that there are my papers and my paints and my drawings, which are like the prints of long, thin fingers made in red. The colours of the creatures inside the Planet of Clay don't have outlines—like the shapes in impressionist art, they are just shades of water ... the eyes and the edges blur and mingle, and the heads too, even the locks of hair ... all swimming in water. And these creatures don't leave, the creatures never grow inside my planet. Each one of these forms has a name and a job. All of this was in my head, I liked that there were circles inside circles inside circles in my head. Stories inside stories. Stories interweaving with stories!

After, a secret planet came along that I could actually touch. I named it my fourth secret planet and I still have it, even though now it is wandering and feverish and is all getting lost, and I don't have the energy to concentrate enough to describe it to you.

My current secret planet, the fourth and final one, I will tell you about along with the story of the siege, even though the story of the siege is held inside the story of Clever Hassan, and also inside the story of the two boys and the cart of herbs. It doesn't matter if we make one story out of two stories, it will be better like that. In the world of colours, this happens too—one colour comes out of two, and the new colour gathers the traits of the two previous colours. We will try it here, in the world of words. It won't do any harm, as long as time comes back and turns into a forest path on a cloud.

It doesn't matter that the stories are circles with intersecting centres, and not just circles coming out of other circles only to separate off and fly away into a more distant sky.

THE COLOUR WASN'T exactly purple. I mean the event that I am going over again with you, when Hassan carried me and my head was dangling over his back. It's the thing I told you about a little while ago, about stories when they turn into circles with intersecting centres (which I learned from mixing colours). That story, when my head was dangling and I was somewhere between just awake and fully awake, is still repeating itself in new circles with the same centre.

I said it wasn't exactly purple. The colour was like the colour of the flying woman in one of the paintings in Sitt Souad's collection. Do you know it? A woman is being carried by a man and she is flying over a city. Perhaps the name of the artist was Chagall, I'm not sure.

Sitt Souad told me about his life and about the history of art. She adored Chagall's paintings and spent hours explaining in minute detail each of the pictures in the leather-bound books I still remember. She said to me that she had collected them throughout her travels, and she had lots of them. I let her talk, and I would close my eyes and think of the meanings of her words and how it was possible that words were colours! This painting was in one of the volumes that I hid in my box. It wasn't just that picture, but lots of pictures by the same artist. I think if it was possible for me to be an artist, I would paint like this man did, he thought about colours in the same way as me! My mother said that Sitt Souad did all this out of pity, and she was angry that all these books were piling up in our house. I felt like I owned a treasure in that picture of the woman flying within a man's embrace! She used to come to me in a dream. I drew the same picture, I drew it over and over, but smaller. I presented one of my copies as a gift to Sitt Souad and she hung it on one of the walls in her house after surrounding it with a brown wooden frame. If

you knew that picture, you would understand what I mean and why I am telling you
about it now. I was hanging with Hassan like
that picture in that purple moment. The difference was that the man was flying with the
woman over the city, and he was wearing
green and the woman was wearing pointed
shoes and a blue dress, and her head wasn't
dangling, her head was flying too! One of
her hands was reaching forward as if they
were swimming, in a unified movement. Sitt
Souad said they were flying and I didn't com-
ment, not even by moving my head, but I
said to myself that they were swimming in
the air over the city.

Hassan and I were swimming too in the
middle of the horrible smells from the bubbles. My head was dangling and so were my
hands, the blue purple colour was the same.
The same colour as the painting.

Do you know Hassan? Perhaps you've got to
know him, or you are one of his friends. He
is a son of Ghouta. That's what he said to me.
I don't know whether he is from Douma,

where my cellar, my last secret planet, is, but he said that he is one of the Shabab Ghouta, and I called him Clever Hassan, like the folk tale. I like this story, I used to read it over and over, and every time it was a different story—every story made Hassan different. But Hassan, in all the stories, is the rescuer and the saviour. Prince or pauper ... he only changes his outward appearance! It's enough to swap your clothes in order to change yourself. Do you know the story of the prince and the pauper? I think it's very funny, how the pauper changes places with the prince. That's how the story goes. I found out later that I was one of the people called *poor*. I wonder, if I swapped feet with another girl, what would happen? Would our deaths be any different?

It would be beautiful if every death had its own colour. Death is a hat that makes colours invisible. I think it would be better to turn mourning occasions into events full of colour, a colour specific to each person who has died. Perhaps we could paint tombstones with the dead person's own colour, which they could decide during their life. That would be hard, making each person think of their own colour, especially if some person puts down colour laws, and we wake up one day and find these laws right there in front of us, telling us what each colour means. Who decides meanings? This really annoys me! But it helps me, thinking of Clever Hassan's colour. What would be the right colour for him? If some paints suddenly appeared in my hand now so I could draw him, what colour would he be? Hassan needs to be drawn directly with colour, he doesn't need a pencil or an eraser, just my paints that are waiting under the bed that I am going back to. I will find Clever Hassan's colour when I have the paints. It will be a mixture of my special colours, which I keep in my secret pages. Colours you don't know. I am using them to get to know my own colour; I will definitely discover it one day. Perhaps when I grow up. This will happen. I will get out of here, and I will go to my paints.

There are two pictures of Hassan in my head, the rest of the few pictures I had of him have disappeared from my memory. One is the image of him carrying me and running while the horrible bubbles fell from the sky and I was noticing the blue-purple colour on the walls and he was shouting at people to keep away from the area of the bombing. And the other, the last image of him, is of when he was raving and jumping about in the cellar after everyone left and I was alone. He was looking at me with a look I know very well, the one that's like a skewer of fire pulling your heart out of your ribs before throwing you on the floor. At that moment, I was standing by the window and looking at the lengthways line of sky that could be seen between the buildings. (This wouldn't have been there if the outside space didn't keep getting enlarged. Day by day, more rectangular segments of sky appear as buildings vanish.) Hassan was gathering some things from the floor of the cellar and shouting at me, saying I needed to get ready to go. He said that he would leave me with some of his relatives, that he wouldn't be able to look after me on a daily basis. *But Saad put his faith in me.* He said that glaring at me between one pace and another.

He meant my brother. My brother's name was Saad. I didn't tell you before, but Hassan kept repeating that phrase. The bombing was getting closer. I thought for the first time in my life that I would live like the other girls. And that I wanted to stay here, with him. With this Clever Hassan. This would be enough for me. And I thought, as well, that I would stop walking, that I could control my feet, and I wanted to stop next to him. I wanted to tell him this and my tongue started moving. I could have done it, I swear on my mother! But I didn't get the chance to speak and tell him that he could untie my hand and let me stand next to him. He was angry and we heard the thunder of the bombing, and my body shrivelled up and I sat on the plastic mat and watched him.

On his left shoulder dangled a medium-sized camera. On the other shoulder, his gun. He said that we would go outside and that I had to cover my head. Just then I looked at him, I wasn't afraid to stare. I memorised his face, and we stayed hanging like that. We—he and I—were hanging, connected by an invisible string that pulled us from the two edges of the world.

Hassan came up to me and then he was facing me. My hair was loose over my body and I stayed standing firm, staring at him. I didn't know what I had to do, but I was rising in the air and I wanted to pray to God that he would stay next to me. I knew then that God is compassionate, perhaps this was what my mother meant when she said that God is compassionate, and Clever Hassan was God's compassion. If it wasn't for that moment, I wouldn't have been able to write to you now.

I reached out my hand to him so he could untie the rope, but he looked at me, confused.

Hassan didn't untie the rope. I was positive that if he had, I would have stayed with him. He went on staring for a few minutes, and his eyes reddened, and the bombing intensified. I was reaching my hand out to him, and he was looking in my eyes. He asked me to be quiet then pulled the rope tight with his teeth. I shook my head that I didn't want that. He pointed to his hand, and I replied with a vehement nod and I kept nodding, so he backed away shouting and began to be hysterical. He kept talking for a while, and I didn't understand much of it because he was swearing and cursing and talking to himself in a muffled voice, but I understood from a few phrases that he would come back for me, and I would be protected by him, and I wasn't to be afraid of anything.

He sat down and took off the black bag he had been carrying and put it in the corner, and linked his hands around his head and lit a cigarette. He was smoking just then. He put the end of the cigarette between his lips as if he wanted to squeeze it, then he knocked the ash off hastily, and his lips were trembling.

The bombing didn't stop but the times between one bomb and the next started to get longer, and Hassan didn't look at me until he had finished his cigarette and thrown it away. I was standing right in front of him.

He moved his entire body in the act of throwing away his cigarette (which vanished behind some packages of paper), and a mouse passed between the bags and disappeared suddenly before he could shoot it.

Hassan actually shot his rifle!

The sound was sudden, but it happened naturally. I used to think that I would go deaf if ever I heard the sound of shooting nearby. But this happened naturally. The bullet landed in front of me, and I stayed in my place, unmoving. My fingers started to twitch and my feet decided to walk, but I walked on the spot. And my head shook. I wanted to go up the stairs but Hassan grabbed hold of me and returned me to my place, and he stroked my hair and apologised, then he hugged me to him. He was still shaking. The sound of the shot was still ringing in my ears. Only his lips trembled and it was difficult for him to get his words out. He sat next to me and carried on with what he was saying. I kept quiet even though my feet were hurting me and I wanted to walk, and he kept on with his stammering. He said he would come back to save me, and I was looking in his eyes and he closed them. Then I put my hand on his hand and he didn't draw it away. He stayed as he was. I felt like I was expanding and growing, and my head was bumping against the ceiling of the cellar, like Alice in Wonderland when she drank the magic potion and ate the cakes. He went on, with closed eyes. I can say to you what he said, simply and easily, and it is the only thing that I remember in such precise detail out of everything that has ever happened in my life, I can even tell you how he moved his eyelashes, but it doesn't matter because I will see him again, and there's no need to bring up more of these details.

I was getting bigger ... I was still growing, and the whole world vanished. I started to overwhelm all the space in the cellar, and he was holding my hand and stuttering, then I squeezed my fingers around his and nodded. He pulled his hand away and backed off, scared! Then he looked at me harshly and went back to jumping away from me, as if he had suddenly woken from a nightmare. He threw the black bags to one side and said *We could die at any moment. I want to take you to a family's house away from here, there's no bombs there. You'll be safe. I'm coming back after a day or two, don't worry ... Agreed? I have to tie you to me ... to my hand ... those were Saad's instructions. I'm not abandoning you. Promise me you'll do what I say!*

He made an agreeing motion with his head, and he looked me in the eye and urged me to do like him. I have held on to those words of his—word ... by word.

I turned my face away and stood still. I pulled the rope from the window, and he shouted again, *You have to listen to me ... you don't have a choice.*

He came up to me, trying to untie the rope from the window, so I pushed him away from me and screamed, then the bombing came back, it was very close to us, and he said *Do you want to die? That's easy to do here ... Let's get out of here, quickly!*

I shook my head.

The bombing came a second time and he said *Just a few minutes and I'll be back, we have to leave at once … I'm taking some pictures … A few minutes and I'll be back … You have to come with me … It's an order, and I can't ignore it!*

Hassan went out.

I intended to unfasten my tie, and I did try to untie the rope while he was gone. I hadn't tried, before that moment, to learn the shapes of the ropes that I've been tied with. I never looked very closely at them, and I didn't try to become familiar with the shape of the red bracelet that the rope marks left behind over the years. They were like pits in my flesh, pale red fading to pink. Even when my mother untied the ropes those traces would be left behind on both wrists, and while my mother kept moving the rope from one hand to the other I didn't even try to touch the red bracelet that the ropes carved across my wrist. Perhaps it had become part of my hand.

Hassan went out of the cellar door, camera in his hand, and the last thing I saw of him was his fingers that vanished when the door closed.

I AM HERE, alone for I don't know how long. I have taken off my shirt and my trousers, and stayed in my long sleeveless shirt. My shirt is yellow and I used to wear it under a short coat, the yellow shirt's job was to cover my behind. It is a shirt, but it is like a dress that reaches to the knee. One of the women gave it to me, along with some black trousers. People here are generous and give others whatever they don't have, especially old clothes. Bundles of old clothes were scattered in the roads, thrown in the street, and mixed with the remnants of the rubbish.

My shirt is new and clean, but it isn't much better than the clothes that my mother used to bring from Souk Al-Haramiya. It's a stained shirt now, but it has kept its colour, which shines in the day when the sunlight falls on it; it looks like fire and it seems like the sun is burning me, but I love seeing the sunshine on it. My mother usually wore colours I didn't like, and she had strange habits of hoarding things. I remember the colours of her clothes precisely, even though all I remember of her face is its dark rosy colour, and that there were waves among her brown and white hair ... She had gone grey early, and grey became the colour of her head, but she didn't colour her hair. She tried it once, and it looked like a black circle topped by a bunch of thin, red, tangled threads. She said that she was too old for red hair, and it was too expensive for us, and anyway it wouldn't change anything in her life! She never did it again, ever. Her concerns over the clothes she slept in made me curious. She was meticulous about ironing her nightclothes, and their colours were bright and sparkling and colourful, and they were clean and ironed for sleeping in. It was something she never did for the clothes she went outside in. I am telling you about my mother's nightclothes and the ray of sunshine and my yellow shirt because she had an abaya of the exact same colour and I remember every detail of it. The colour of the yellow abaya was the same as the yellow when the rays of sunshine reach my shirt from the cellar window, but the feel of the cloth is different, my fingers can tell. That nightdress stayed hanging in our house until last year, when my mother turned it into little rags for cleaning the house.

I have to be alert in case I hear any movement, to put on my clothes so Hassan doesn't see me in this embarrassing state. I will have time to move before he comes down. I will hear his footsteps.

I have been lying down for a whole day. I feel better because of the yellow shirt and its colours under the sunlight. Even though my head spins sometimes, and it whirls me round while I am sleeping, my head is the centre of a circle and everything is turning around it. I dozed off twice while my head went round and I woke up with a sharp headache. The cellar was filled with shadows, and outside the sky had a strange light; I didn't see the moon, perhaps we are at the beginning of the new month when the full moon disappears. The sky lights up the shadows of things here, and something was crawling between my thighs, but it was soft and small and there was no call to be afraid. It was tickling me and there was no need to discover what it was, because it was hardly touching my body. And I felt some damp, and a delicious coolness that made me wake up to one more day, and I have been able to regain my strength. This energy is responsible for making me notice that, apart from the colour of my yellow shirt, there is no colour around me other than black and white, not even the rays of the sun! Do you know, in the book of Al-Tha'alibi there is a chapter called "On Varieties of Colours and their Attributes"? And imagine, in that chapter he was explaining the meaning of the colours, and black and white have a different importance to the rest of the colours. In that moment, when I was regaining my energy after getting undressed, I realised that what I had read in that chapter was true. There are dozens of qualities in the colour white, and every quality has its own word that makes me think of a different white. Do you, like me, understand what that means? It means that I can paint infinite colours from one colour: white. *Hijan*—unstained; a noble white camel. *Khalis*—pure. *Nasi'*—flawless. *Yaqaq*—dazzling, brilliant; like white cotton. *Lahiq*—a white bull. *Wadih*—clear. Lots of words that Al-Tha'alibi wrote meaning *white* I don't remember now. I used to memorise them, along with the meanings of the words attached to them. Even my name is one of the shades of white; it's a gazelle! I looked for it in this book, and my name was one of the meanings and qualities of the colours.

During the day I play with the meanings of white. At night I play with the meanings of black, and that is harder because I am not able to write at night. The black of night is somewhere between *adlam* (that is an intense black) and *zall*, or shadow, a murky black that takes its colour from the dust. Relief comes at dawn. I used to believe that dawn would be blue, but this black was *ahwa*, that is the colour between black and red. That came as a surprise. I can't remember all the meanings of the colours anymore. I learned them by heart from that book, and for each and every attribute I made a picture, and as you might have guessed they are still hidden in my box … The book is there too. Even though I have forgotten a lot of its words, it is the only book I ever made use of in my paintings. The meanings and the descriptions would help me to draw, and when I decided to make changes to the story of *Alice in Wonderland*, I drew from it. I will tell you all about it. I am completely awake now and I feel better. I thought that the only thing missing from Alice's journey through Wonderland was some flying fish. If I had lived when the story was written, I would have suggested to the writer that he should add a group of fish fly-ing down the forest path that Alice walks along. Fish appearing and disappearing, cir-cling Alice's head like fairies, and letting out bubbles into the sky over the forest. These bubbles should be coloured, and each fish would make bubbles in its own particular colour, and these would be the lights of the forest that were missing in the story. They could vanish and reappear from time to time, and out of the wings that the fish use to fly with, water could emerge in the shape of little fountains rising up then slipping back into the mouths of the fish that carry their sea under their wings ... This would make the story complete. I drew the fish that I had decided to add to the story of Alice, and I made use of the book of Al-Tha'alibi when I was looking for the qualities of each colour so I could give a name to each fish and picture. There were only four fish, and they are also waiting for me in my box under the bed. In lots of the stories I drew, I added what I would have liked to suggest. In the story of the Little Prince, if I was the writer, I would have liked to add another group of planets, all different sizes, planets that are giant clocks surrounding the Little Prince's planets, and the sound of the ticking second hands is what drives their orbits around themselves. Imagine a group of giant planets that look like clocks, with hands and bells dangling from them ... It would be enough for the prince to pass by them very quickly. I think there is a relationship of some kind between the clock planets and the Little Prince's planets ... I will complete that story if I can. I only drew the giant clocks, and they are still in my box.

I THOUGHT THAT I would walk again and move and hold on to my energy after I woke up to the black and white, but it only lasted for a few hours; I am writing less now. You must have noticed that I'm not drawing the letters like I did before. I can't, I am afraid that my one blue pen will run out, but please don't forget the drawings of each letter that I used at the beginning. I don't think I'll go back to writing in that alphabet before Hassan comes back and I leave this place, but I would like to remind you of my special alphabet that I used to write a large collection of my illustrated stories. My brother found it hard to read, until I wrote it out on a special page with an explanation and coloured it in. He read a batch of stories and he was always interested in reading what I wrote and drew

each day. Until he forgot. I watched him forget in silence. I will try and put it down in the
same way I explained it to my brother:

ا *Alif* ends with a bird with one wing.

ب *Ba'* ends with a bird with two wings.

ت *Ta'* ends with a matchstick.

ث *Tha'* has a lampshade above its three dots.

س *Sin* ends with a bed with tall bedposts.

ج ح خ *Djim* and *Ha'* and *Kha'* end with fingers.

د ذ *Dal* and *Dhal* end with a bow crossed in the
middle by an arrow with a triangle at the
end.

ر ز *Ra'* and *Zay* end with a crescent moon.

ع غ *'Ayn* and *Ghayn* end with a flower with
four petals.

ط ظ ض *Ta'* and *Za'* and *Daad* end with a snake.

ل *Lam* finishes like a small boy with a scarf around his neck. The scarf is flying in the air and the boy is sitting on a small planet.

م *Mim* ends with a sailboat.

ن *Nun* has a sun over the dot.

ه *Ha'* is topped with a hat and a butterfly.

و *Waw* ends with a large eye with long lashes.

ي *Ya'* is topped by the smile of a cat with mustachios.

This is my alphabet, which you probably noticed I used when I wrote before, but now I have stopped. I only use it at the ends of the letters. When the letters come at the beginning or the middle of a word, I write them normally ... This makes the word swim in the white of the page. Don't you agree? I feel better, and I remembered my alphabet! Despite the heat and the blaze of the burning sun, and the nights I had to take off my clothes so they wouldn't stick to my body, and the red spots that are still burning me.

My mother has often come during these nights that I am naked, her face in the dreams is blurry but I know it is my mother. She stands next to me and ties my wrist to her wrist then she runs and drags me with her, and I am rolling along behind her and I don't scream.

At night I open the buttons of my skirt. My chest is big as ever and it weighs on my body. My skin hasn't changed but it has begun to feel sticky and it tastes bitter. I relish the drops of sweat that slide over my body. I am able to drink from my body. I wipe my sweating stomach with my hand then I suck my fingers, but the taste is salty and it makes my throat even drier. In the day the colour of my body turns to red. Swollen red spots have started to emerge on my stomach. I could feel them last night, while I was looking at the window. The dog, who used to come close to the window now and then, didn't appear even though I was waiting for him. Hassan told me that this area was dangerous and it faced continual bombing. No one came near it. It's been two days since I heard the thunder of bombs, so why don't the people appear? I don't think I am able to scream again. I have to scream! And I have to write in the day and pinch my ear and bite my tongue to prove that I am still alive.

I was nibbling three bites of the last apple, which had been red and was now completely shrivelled but I could chew its grains for a long time and I enjoyed how bitter it was. One more day and the apple will be finished. It was the last one from the bag that Hassan brought. I put on my second shirt, and I hid the apple underneath, next to my stomach. But in the morning the yellow shirt was soaked in water. I had sweated a lot in the night and the apple had rolled and come to rest under my feet.

I need to separate my skin from the shirt, and the insects that circle around me have begun to annoy me and bite me. I peed in my clothes in the night, and everything inside me is burning. Between my thighs feels like it has been ironed. The flies disappeared, and small soft flying insects have appeared in their place. They weren't hovering around me all the time, they would move like a single lump in a few different places, but I woke up one morning, I can't remember when this was anymore, and the lump of soft insects was directly over my head, I even ate one of them and coughed hard. I swallowed an insect when I breathed; it had been between my lips while I was sleeping. I was afraid, and after swallowing the insect and almost choking I stayed awake the next night. And Hassan hasn't come, his face has finally vanished from my mind and now I am only worried about my yellow shirt and the feel of my skin that has turned into a lake brimming with red spots and the burning skin of my head that I scratch during the times I am awake, times which are becoming shorter and shorter. I sleep for long periods and I wake for a short time; I am not able to write down every detail for you anymore. I had more stories and I meant to circle back around my earlier stories, like the little mirrors in the fairy ball, but that's too hard now. I am exhausted and my yellow shirt burns my skin along with the drops of sweat and the blazing sunshine during the day. Still, I am lying down today looking at the plastic mat whose colour has disappeared and the only thing that shows is the colour of dust. Still, I was looking at my body lying on the thin sponge mattress and it was strange—I saw it for the first time and I realised that I am not as ugly as the reflection I see in people's eyes when they look at me. Something strange was going on. I have begun to feel a numbness in my feet and I can't even move them anymore. I think I am fine and all I need is a few drops of water in my dried-up throat. I will put on the black jacket again—perhaps Hassan will come suddenly.

I SLEPT FOR a long time, and I don't know what the plane did but I see dust in the sky. I know it's possible for the man sitting inside the plane to look at the ground and see houses. I drew houses in the shape of people sleeping, and mountains in the same way too. The mountains were sleeping more deeply than the houses. The houses had ears and lips and the mountains had huge noses and bulging eyes. All I thought was how the eyes of the houses and the mountains were looking at the planes and not the other way around!

Have you ever tried to draw a sleeping mountain, with a plane above and a house below? Just an ordinary house, not the kind of houses we draw in stories. I thought of a house made from two parallel lines. Its walls are made of glass. If this house came out of my pages now and I began to form it, it wouldn't be like the house we lived in, or the houses next to it, or the alleyways I knew. One house. Walls not attached to anything, so there is no hearing the neighbours while they pee and shout and poo. The house I want will be like Sitt Souad's library. Its walls made of glass. I will paint them all. I will tell Hassan, when he comes back, what I am thinking about. I will leave some space between the glass walls and the bookshelves to let in the light that will pass through the colours, and I will be there under the bookshelves and among the heroes of the books lined up so neatly, and there will be lots of packs of paper ... and colouring pens.

Now the plane is hovering in the sky.

The plane doesn't know what I'm thinking about.

The man sitting in the plane is looking at the house, or maybe he's not looking.

How do houses look from the sky?

Will the houses just be grey colours?

I would have told you the story of the siege that Hassan told me, but I can't bring back to mind the details of what he said. He came that time when I was growing and expanding like Alice. I think I am losing my ability to concentrate again.

I think about books and what I need to write during this long time ... so long it never ends ...

It's been two days since I have written anything.

Colours are flying out of me, and I am on my secret Planet of Clay now, and I think of Hassan's fingers on the door as he slams it shut.

I heaved myself up two days ago and I was walking in the cellar, walking and walking, and I was knocking the window bars and the knot didn't come undone. I circled into the corners and around the packs of paper, my blue pen in my hand. It is on the verge of running out, but it still writes. I carry it and walk, and I stuff it into the gap between the rope and my wrist and I try to break the tie, but it doesn't break. I walk quickly. I jump over the paper. I look at the empty street, then at the cellar floor. It was a single cement block, unpaved. Dust has started to cover everything here, even the small sponge pillow that burns my neck in the heat, and the plastic mat, and the packs of paper. I find a paper knife and I tear open a cardboard pack and scatter the white pages over the cellar floor, and it looks much brighter so I carry on scattering pages. I dig in the wall with the rusty paper knife I found among the cardboard boxes, and the squeak of it cheers me up. The lines are white on the cement wall. I draw easily, I dig the wall easily, here on the wall I draw fear easily too. Perhaps I am imagining it now, I am not sure, but I imagine that writing is just fear, and I can't find a colour for fear. Is there a phrase that can describe the colour that the chemical bombs left behind them? Was it blue? Grey with tinges of blue?

Was it transparent and blue? I called the colour purple. But was it really? The colour of water when it is a mixture of blue and green? Is it the same colour as the traces of gas on the walls of the houses? … Is this the colour of fear?

Will I disappear? Will I die?

My legs won't stop walking in the cellar.

I am tired.

I can't stop walking.

My body bumps into the walls and my feet don't stop.

Here everything spinning around me is grey, even the two little boys! They were grey. Didn't I tell you their story? Perhaps I forgot. I feel a dryness in my throat. But being awake has come back!

The two boys came a few days ago, repeatedly. I didn't dare call them at first. But I did a few days ago, and when they saw me they ran away. I watched them for days while they were passing through the alley and wheeling a small wooden cart, I listened to their discussions and their whispers. I think one of them was ten and the other was younger. The older boy carried a stick on his back and he had tied it with a rope like a rifle. The stick was thin. It was a tree branch with twigs twisting round its middle, but there was one small twig that stuck out at a right angle.

The older boy put his finger on the twig that stuck out at a right angle and they would laugh. The wooden cart was filled with herbs. It had three wheels. The front wheel was huge while the two back wheels were smaller. Why were they filling the cart with herbs? Hassan said that people were eating wild herbs. He said that the siege was hard, and the two boys seemed to be laughing as they moved among the rubble. They were two little men, not boys—how can I explain it to you? They were moving lightly, their bodies moved like men, but they were just boys. I discovered them on a hot morning. The mornings here are stifling too, and the sky is blue. Rays of sunshine were coming in through the window I was tied to. I reached out my fingers and they disappeared. It's true, they disappeared and I woke up to the clatter of the boys moving around in the alley in front of the destroyed building.

The rays of sunshine, although they burn, provide me with life. The specks that show up in the luminous rays brush against my cheeks.

The movement of the boys and the rays of sunshine made me jump. They were in the building next to the one that the dog had taken the hand from. The smaller boy was in between the iron rods that stuck out of the rubble like snakes. These weren't like the snakes in *The Little Prince*. The older boy was digging and he brought out some pots and pans then threw them to one side. The smaller boy gathered some of the iron rods and put them in his lap. Then he laughed and waved at his brother (I supposed he was his brother) as he said *Immek will buy some bread with this*.

Then he jumped about and joy flooded his face.

The older boy laughed. He was wearing blue trousers and a red shirt, the colours shone in the sunlight. The smaller one had dirty clothes, his top half was almost bare and he was skinny. His T-shirt was tight and showed his stomach. His body, and his hair too, were filled with dust as he dived into the rubble, then he threw the iron rods away as he dusted his hands off and grabbed a handful of the herbs (I think it was chicory). As he chewed it, he looked at the cellar and headed towards me. The window glass was broken and he was looking through it, so I hid against the wall. I stuck to it. I could have asked them for help, knocked on the wall. My tongue stood still. I would have closed my eyes again if they had left but their insistence on knowing what was inside the cellar kept me pinned against the wall and I stopped breathing. The silence was harsh and there wasn't a trace of a plane in the sky. There wasn't even the buzzing of mosquitos. Just three large flies hovering in the cellar, making a hum. One of the flies was big and almost blue or blue green, it looked giant in this place. Perhaps it has something to eat. The younger boy reached his head inside and was looking ahead at the pile of cardboard packages. If he had looked down at the wall he would have discovered me, but he drew back and said *There's nothing here.* The other one replied irritably, *Yalla ... let's get back before Immek goes mad!*

Of course they were brothers, the resemblance between them was obvious. I heard the rods clanking on top of the cart they were slowly dragging, then I raised my head again. I think I was moving like a lizard on the wall. Then I watched them as they disappeared into the alleyway, and some of the iron rods fell off the cart so the big one came back for them and he held the stick in front of him and swung it round in every direction like the men here do with their guns, and his brother yelled at him to help him with the heavy cart. And in a few minutes they disappeared.

The second time, they passed by quickly and didn't stop. There weren't many herbs and grasses in the cart this time, and they were running as they pulled it along.

The third and last time, the cart was filled with iron rods, and there was a change! They had painted the cart green, it looked like the colour I used to choose when I mixed blue and dark green together. This colour was distributed over the side of the cart, but not very well, some gaps appeared where the old brown colour showed through. They had not painted it very skilfully. But the cart seemed new and different. And the wheel spokes were painted light blue. They were decorated with strips of white plastic, plastic bags cut up into soft ropes and wound around into the shapes of flowers. The herbs in the cart were piled up with their roots attached and there was soil hanging off them. Sunlight had made the roots wither. In both the previous times the roots had been cut ... perhaps the herbs were a type of mallow this time ... I wasn't sure. But they were shouting as they went past, the little one seemed angry, and soil fell from the cart. There was a plane, I heard it. But then the sound went away. The two boys watched the sky. The little one tripped and fell and the big one laughed spitefully, making the little one even angrier. Their skinniness was odd to me. I was losing my energy and I decided to shout to them. I shook the window and stammered. My voice came out of me ... My shout was loud, and they froze in their tracks. I reached out my hand to them, I waved my hand, and I tried to reach out with the other one that was tied to the window. They were nailed to the spot. The light outside seemed to have made me invisible. I was shouting and knocking on the wall and they were nailed to the spot ... I heard the sharp scream that came out of my throat, and I felt my terror increase because this sound that came out of me frightened me. The little one yelled *It's a monster!*

The big one scolded him: *There are no monsters here. Immi said it's the dogs, because they are starving. Be quiet ... Come on.*

He took his brother's hand and aimed his stick in the direction where I was shouting from, then he moved it towards me and yelled *Tak-tak-tak*. He was aiming the stick at me and I fell on the floor!

He said to his brother, *Look! There's nothing there.*

I became even more terrified when he said that so I stood up again and felt a pain in my chest, and I started shouting again, so the two of them ran and the stick fell. The big one shouted *My rifle! My rifle!*

He came back to pick it up, and they ran off with the cart and disappeared.

In the next few days they will disappear completely. Even so, I saw their fingers and those small hands of theirs. They were just like my hands, moving strangely as if they were going to escape their bodies. Probably, the boys already know about the secret of hands. Probably, they share in the secret, along with me, that hands take precedence over tongues, and fingers over lips. Their fingers moved like dancing feet. I was watching my fingers after the boys vanished. Both of my hands speak. My feet walk and get angry and hate. My hands are connected, they talk with rope. I draw with them. I had to discover that the secret of hands isn't only that they move. They are capable of creating their own independent existence. In this way, each part of my body is independent from the other parts, each part of my body forms its own being—not in my head where the Planet of Clay is, and not in my feet which are turning into a brain, and not in my fingers which are turning into a tongue, but in each part directly. Recently my heart went somewhere else, it left its place. The weight of the left side of my chest disappeared and there was an empty space. Strange that I am talking to you about two boys dragging a wooden cart underneath a sky and a plane, and what made them disappear, and then I shift to the disappearance of my heart and of Hassan, who went out to take pictures of the bombs and didn't come back.

The older boy, who looked in the cellar with horror after hearing my scream, didn't cry, he took his brother's hand and set off running with the cart that tripped up, and then they fell. I told you these details a little earlier, you will feel I am repeating myself but you are starting to know my theory now, about circular stories with intersecting centres which are only completed by retellings and new details.

As I told you, they ran and the colours disappeared with them. Since that moment I haven't seen any new colours, since the moment the boys disappeared.

But really, now I am thinking ... where are the two boys, and where do they live?

Do they believe I am just a ghost? Why don't more people pass along this lane? Where did the people disappear to?

Perhaps the two boys will tell someone about me. Do I wait for Hassan, or do I go with them?

I will be lost from Hassan if I go with them, but I have stopped caring about such details. What I care about now are the two colourful boys. They will come back, I will teach them how to paint the cart properly and how to mix colours.

They ran quickly when they ran away. Do they have a family? They have a mother. Or maybe their family will disappear like everyone did for me. Didn't Um Saeed turn into a half statue made of clay? Perhaps they were made of paper and have been scattered by fire and bombs. I know they are afraid, and that they run. Isn't it possible that they will turn into clay statues, as happened to Um Saeed? Is Um Saeed still there … a semi-body? So we are not made of just clay alone, but of paper, like drawing paper, and this body and these hands of mine can turn into a collection of paper shreds. Why do bombs turn bodies into little pieces?

An annoying movement of a fly over my head! But the flies in front of me are stuck.

The flies hanging over a black point seem to be glued. How did they get stuck? There is no glue around here. Everything here is hard and dry.

The fly is stuck. It isn't like Um Saeed's body— it isn't breaking up. But it is stuck and it buzzes ... Zzzzzz ... Zzzzzz ... Its wings are blue. No ... its body is blue. Do we say the *body* of a fly? Do they have a body? You know that I am not experienced at language, although I used to love reading the way I love my colours, but I'm not sure what we call the middle of a fly. In any case, it was blue tinged with green.

In this place, there is nothing except the flies and me.

The flies are keeping me company; we contemplate each other. And the dog who passes from time to time keeps me company also. I see him but he doesn't see me. The flies see me. We—the dog, the three large flies, and me—we five beings live here.

The first fly is stuck, and what it is stuck over is strange. Just a point, like the point on a triangle. It's a drop of blood, between the edges of the packs of paper and the edge of the wall. The fly is stuck there. I can separate one of its wings from its body and I see what can be done to each of the lumps surrounding us. My limbs are unified and they hold together, they don't come apart, but the limbs of others around me come apart very easily, and it could be that the same thing will happen here. The first wing can be pulled off easily, then the second wing—that's how I pulled both of them off. There isn't even a sound for the process of tearing the wings. This is a big, disgusting fly! How is it possible that it disgusts me so much when I pull off its wings; they are coloured too, though not completely. The colour is in the middle. The wings are transparent. They have fine, delicate black veins running through them, as if they were drawn on with a tiny feather. I can see my fingers through the first transparent wing. The second wing, which I pulled off slowly, is decorated with fine, even more delicate lines. I crushed the wings very easily between two fingers, and they turned into white dust ... into nothing ... the substance vanished, and what remained of the fly began to move slowly. It was a lump of shiny blue colour. How did its small, delicate legs get caught in a drop of sticky blood? Perhaps it isn't blood, perhaps it is part of the shit scattered on the walls. The blue-green lump that the fly turned into will soon become nothing. Disappearing is such an easy process! Half of Um Saeed's body used to move around beneath her chest, and then suddenly it was somewhere else. Why did the top half remain whole? How did that strange fluke happen?

The fly slowly lost its movements, and I watched it, crammed into the corner between the piled-up packs of paper and the wall, right before my eyes.

The other two flies disappeared for a few minutes then reappeared by the window. I will pull off their wings, but I won't rub them with my fingers, their colours are beautiful, especially those dark green veins distributed over the light blue film. I don't understand why that fly came here and abandoned its friends, then plunged into that drop of dried blood. And then that drop itself ... whose blood is it?

I AM HUNGRY.

The numbness has risen to my knees.

I am hungry.

My throat is dry.

There is no water here and no food, the last
bit of apple dried out and I swallowed it along
with its seeds, as I think I told you. The two
flies came back towards me, they are hovering over my head now, but I can't move my
hand very high. I want to go back to the window, I want to take a look at the alley, maybe
the two boys will pass by ...

I am trying to tell you all the details and I am failing. I have lost the energy I had left, I am trying to tell you every small detail of the stories, but I can't.

My fingers have been hurting me for a few days … What would you do if you were in my place?

Maybe I have been here for two or three months, perhaps less, perhaps more. I don't remember the last time I ate … a red apple Hassan brought … There was a bag of fruit! But I ate the apple … Its seeds were bitter in my throat, but what I like most about the apple is the seeds.

HOW MANY DAYS have passed?

Why did I stop pulling out the threads from my hijab? I used to pull out a thread every day, and I can't remember now when I stopped doing it. The hijab was thin and I could easily pull out the threads that I needed, but I stopped. How could I forget to do that? How did time escape me? It is the thing I need the most right now. But I am too weak to get up. I ate the last things left here, a few rotten potatoes and onions I found behind a pack of paper when I was walking and walking between the walls of the cellar. Only my hands are in front of me now. My fingers are in front of my eyes. The redness that the rope has left around my wrist is getting bigger; it burns me because I pulled the rope until it stripped off my skin and blood came out from under the knot, and nothing I tried worked in untying it.

Yesterday I beat the window bars with my head and tried to break the knot, but Hassan had tied it tightly. I used the edge of the rusty paper knife to scrape the rope but it was no use. The colour of the rope became grey; it was thick and relentless.

I tried to nick a piece off the rope with the paper knife, but the rope seems like iron. Not a single atom of it is crumbling!

Yesterday night the rusty paper knife broke in two.

Today one of the pieces cut my finger and blood came out. I wrapped my finger with a strip I tore off the yellow shirt, and the strip was dyed blood colour, and its yellow turned into purple.

I WRITE TO you and I sleep on my stomach. I need a long time to assemble the words. My fingers don't move. The small insects hover in the room. My bed has become damp, and there is the same smell here as in the school toilets my mother used to clean. The smell is sharper here, and I still have the smaller piece of the paper knife I can use to scrape the thick rope that has itself turned into a knife on the skin of my hand. I look out of the corner of my eyes at the cellar window, and see a piece of sky. Perfect blue. No roar of planes, no thunder of explosions, total silence in the height of the afternoon, and my head is spinning and the walls are moving around me and they come right up to me like they did in Sitt Souad's library. The Little Prince is sitting next to me, and his planets are in his hand. Then he puts his hand on the knot of the thick rope and everyone lines up around him, Alice and the elephants and the Cheshire Cat and the White Rabbit and the red fox and the snake. They are here, and I am looking out of the corner of my eye at the piece of sky and at the characters. I am trying to move my hand in the air but I can't lift it, and I am writing to you with the other hand, but it is shaking.

THE FLOOR OF the cellar is filled with white pages. I scattered them all. My coloured pages hover around my head. They came out of my box and are flying around among the Prince's planets. I watch them moving like on a television screen.

I can't focus. I am hungry. Perhaps the boys will come back with the cart of herbs.

My stories aren't finished and the story of Hassan is still at the beginning.

The story of my mother who disappeared.

The story of the bald girl who disappeared.

The story of my brother who disappeared.

The story of Um Saeed who disappeared.

The story of Hassan who disappeared.

The story of the two boys who disappeared.

The dog who disappeared.

The flies who disappeared.

I am a story, I too will disappear (or maybe I am with you now as you read my scattered words) like the Cheshire Cat did in the story of Alice.

My fingers are shaking again. The pen hasn't run out yet but the blue has faded. Some of the letters disappear and I rewrite them ... Perhaps I will stop at any moment.

I feel like my eyes have a small ant running over them. An ant came out of them and it stops me from seeing, and seeing is brown, like the colour of the ant, and the ant is spreading over my head. We went out to go to the house of the lady my mother cleans for, and who taught me to read and write, and who made me what I am, we just went out ...

We went out in a small white bus.

It was just a short journey, like ones we had made dozens of times before.

My throat is dry.

My head is spinning.

I can't focus on the letters anymore.

And I must scream ...

LERI PRICE is an award-winning literary translator of contemporary Arabic fiction. Price's translation of Khaled Khalifa's *Death Is Hard Work* was a finalist for the 2019 National Book Award for Translated Literature (US) and winner of the 2020 Saif Ghobash Banipal Prize for Arabic Literary Translation. Her translation of Khaled Khalifa's *No Knives in the Kitchens of This City* was short-listed for the ALTA National Translation Award. Price's other recent translations include *Sarab* by award-winning writer Raja Alem.

On the Design

As book design is an integral part of the reading experience, we would like to acknowledge the work of those who shaped the form in which the story is housed.

Tessa van der Waals (Netherlands) is responsible for the cover design, cover typography, and art direction of all World Editions books. She works in the internationally renowned tradition of Dutch Design. Her bright and powerful visual aesthetic maintains a harmony between image and typography and captures the unique atmosphere of each book. She works closely with internationally celebrated photographers, artists, and letter designers. Her work has frequently been awarded prizes for Best Dutch Book Design.

On this cover, the text is dynamically positioned on a photograph snapped by the cover designer herself, Tessa van der Waals. The author's name allows for a prominent placement of the characteristic capital *Y* of the CA Oskar typeface, a typeface that was first developed for the Traumzeit music festival in Germany.

The cover has been edited by lithographer Bert van der Horst of BFC Graphics (Netherlands).

Suzan Beijer (Netherlands) is responsible for the typography and careful interior book design of all World Editions titles.

The text on the inside covers and the press quotes are set in Circular, designed by Laurenz Brunner (Switzerland) and published by Swiss type foundry Lineto.

All World Editions books are set in the typeface Dolly, specifically designed for book typography. Dolly creates a warm page image perfect for an enjoyable reading experience. This typeface is designed by Underware, a European collective formed by Bas Jacobs (Netherlands), Akiem Helmling (Germany), and Sami Kortemäki (Finland). Underware are also the creators of the World Editions logo, which meets the design requirement that "a strong shape can always be drawn with a toe in the sand."